CHAPTER ONE

STANLEY Maddox finished speaking and rested his hands together on the top of his desk. He stared at the girl sitting opposite him, waiting for her to speak. But shock seemed to have struck her dumb. Understandably, he thought, for he had reacted similarly when he had read the letter from the detective agency at the weekend.

'I don't suppose there could possibly be a mistake?' she said finally.

'No.' He leaned back in his chair, tall, spare, and grey-haired. 'The business Mr Saville's great-great-grandfather started when he emigrated to America is still in existence, though Mr Saville has never had any personal connection with it. He inherited his shares from his father—probably kept them out of sentiment as they're not worth much,' he added with a slight smile. 'The company keep a list of all their shareholders and their addresses, so from there on it was plain sailing.'

'I wish I'd never found those letters,' Susan Andrews said forcefully. 'It would have been better for the Wentworth line to become extinct than be carried on by a man like Gregg Saville.'

Her mind went back to that fateful day, three months ago, when she had gone down to Brocklehurst—home of the Dukes of Wentworth for the past three hundred and fifty years—with a man from Sothebys, who had been asked to make an inventory and valuation of the contents for probate.

'Start in the attic,' they had been instructed by the Duchess. 'It's full of rubbish as far as I know, but there may be something of value that's been overlooked.'

As it happened there wasn't, and by the time they had reached the old trunk in the far corner of the vast room, and found nothing but a jumble of old clothes inside, they had nearly closed the lid again and written it off as one more item for the dustmen. But her lawyer's training had taught her not to accept anything at face value, and while her companion had moved downstairs, Susan had taken out each garment, inspecting it carefully for some trinket of jewellery that might have been pinned there and forgotten. It was all ladies' aparrel, dating back about a hundred years or so, well preserved, but smelling musty. She had breathed a sigh of relief when she had reached the last garment, a pure silk dressing gown. It looked like new, the colour and appliqué so delicate that she had lifted it out with the intention of asking the Duchess if she might keep it. Certainly the loose wrap-around style was as fashionable today as it had been then. But as she draped it against her, a small package had fallen out of one of the sleeves and dropped to the floor. It was a bundle of letters, tied with lavender ribbon.

Since she assumed them to be love letters, a natural curiosity had prompted her to read them, and her surprise at learning who had written them was as great as her surprise today on learning who the writer's great-great-grandson was.

Dated 1820, and sent to a post-restante address in a nearby town, they were from Lord Henry Saville, and written to his favourite sister. Youngest son of the seventh Duke of Wentworth, he had been banished and disinherited by his parents because of marriage to a farm labourer's daughter. He had emigrated to America, and because his name was forbidden to be spoken, and all portraits and memorabilia of him destroyed, by the time two generations had passed he had disappeared from memory as if he had never existed.

The correspondence covered a period of ten years, by which time he had become fairly affluent, purchasing the brewery where he had first humped beer barrels after arriving penniless in Chicago. He had stopped writing when his sister had died of influenza, and it was easy to conclude that they were her clothes packed away in the trunk, together with the letters that her family had also assumed to be love letters.

And now, because of the tragic and untimely death of his great-great-nephew Charles Saville, tenth Duke of Wentworth, another great-great-nephew, Gregg Saville, owner of the best-selling 'girlie' magazine in the world, had inherited the title and estate.

'Perhaps the shock of learning he's the Duke of Wentworth might give him the impetus to change his way of life,' Stanley Maddox was speaking again.

'You don't really believe that, do you?' Susan asked sceptically. 'From what I've read of him, he revels in his way of life, and if he wanted to change it, there's nothing stopping him. He's made a fortune from that dreadful magazine of his.'

'Owning *Playmate* is certainly not the ideal occupation for a scion of one of England's noblest families,' the solicitor agreed. 'And his reputation as a playboy doesn't help either. But we shouldn't prejudge him. As the Wentworth family's solicitors— and his too for the moment—our duty is to be completely unbiased.' He regarded her gravely over the top of his gold-rimmed glasses. 'I hope you will bear that in mind, Susan, particularly as it's been decided that you should go to Los Angeles to tell Mr Saville of his inheritance.'

'Me?' She looked surprised. 'But surely one of the senior partners would be more suitable?'

'You are the most senior available for the moment. Mr Forbes can't fly because of his heart condition, and Jonathan and I,' he named his nephew, 'have the Wiley fraud case starting at the Old Bailey next Monday. In any case, with your family still tenants on the estate, your knowledge of it is more up to date than ours.'

'I don't see the relevance,' she ventured. 'I can't see him wanting to live at Brocklehurst and run the estate. He'll probably sell it off to the highest bidder.'

'Sir William Royston would be delighted to buy it.' He named an industrialist, famous not only for his financial wizardry but for his philanthropic nature. 'He'd keep the land and give the house to the National Trust. He's also prepared to give certain guarantees to protect the rights of the existing tenants, of whom I believe your father is still one?' Susan nodded, and he continued. 'Naturally, selling the estate is not as satisfactory as keeping it in the family, but in this case it would probably be the best solution.'

'Do you want me to advise Mr Saville of Sir William's offer?'

'I've not had it confirmed in writing yet, so for the moment I think it's better to say nothing.' He hitched forward in his chair. 'Mr Saville—I still can't think of him as the Duke—is sure to want to come and visit Brocklehurst, and we'll have plenty of time to discuss it with him then.'

'When do you want me to leave?' asked Susan.

'Saturday. That will give you Sunday to recover from any jet lag, and have your mind perfectly clear when you meet Mr Saville on Monday. Miss Baker is seeing to your ticket and hotel reservation,' he told her, referring to his secretary.

'I hope Mr Saville knows I'm coming? I'd hate to travel five thousand miles and find he wasn't there!'

'The detective agency is arranging it for us, though

naturally they won't reveal why you want to see him. I don't want the press to get hold of the story until you've met him personally. It's just the kind of thing they love, and because of the part you played in finding him, we'll be dragged into it as well.'

'We might pick up a few clients!' Susan joked. 'After all, we're not allowed to advertise!'

'Fortunately, Maddox, Forbes and Maddox have no need to tout for business.' Where the law was concerned, Stanley Maddox had little sense of humour. He picked up a folder from the desk in front of him. 'I'd like you to read through this. It's a fairly comprehensive report on Mr Saville, and I think you'll find it interesting.

Susan smiled, showing a set of even white teeth. 'I must admit that everything I know about him has been gleaned from the gossip columns. He spends about three months of the year in Europe, and features in them quite often.'

The corners of the solicitor's thin lips quirked in the suspicion of a smile. 'So I gather. The detective agency have included several items from the American newspapers they thought might be of interest.'

Susan stood up and went to the door. Tall and slender, she moved with the perfect co-ordination of an athlete. 'How long do you think I'll be away?' she asked.

'Not more than a week. It might take that time to settle some of the queries.' He shifted slightly in his chair. 'It's very hot in Los Angeles at this time of year, so get yourself a few light things and charge it to the firm. Regard it as an advance on your Christmas bonus!'

That was certainly a surprise, Susan thought to herself. Whatever else one could say about Maddox, Forbes and Maddox, they were not renowned for their open-handedness.

Walking briskly down the corridor to her own small office at the far end, she glimpsed patches of grey, rainwashed sky, through the narrow windows that ranged along one side. They afforded her a picture of the street below: treeless, traffic-clogged, and litter-strewn. It did not change whatever the season, and she thought longingly of the days when she had lived in the country with her parents, and had only come to London for shopping trips. Now London was her home, and a visit to the countryside was regarded as an outing. If only time did not have a habit of changing one's attitudes as well as one's circumstances, she mused, then pushed aside all personal thoughts as she settled down behind her desk and opened the folder.

Lying on the top was a photograph of Gregg Saville; the man who, because of the untimely death of a distant and unknown relative, was now sole heir to the title, fortune and estates of Charles William Henry Arthur Saville, tenth duke of Wentworth. The first thing that struck her was the resemblance to his illustrious ancestors in the portraits in the Long Gallery at Brocklehurst. It was quite remarkable, though she had to admit he was much better looking: narrow slanting eyes beneath thick blond brows, thrusting hair that sprang back from a high, wide brow, a straight nose and extremely determined chin. The mouth was thin but well-shaped, and curved in a sensual smile, though she could well imagine it becoming as uncompromisingly harsh as the rest of his features if he were displeased.

But that probably did not happen too often, for he was a man who appeared to have everything he wanted. He had become a dollar millionaire in his mid-twenties when, after college, he had gone to work for a little read but highly admired Arts magazine. It had not taken him long to find a solution to their circulation problem: nudes. Interspersing them lavishly between the more serious contributions, he found an unbeatable formula for success.

Now there were eight foreign language editions, and in spite of many imitators since its inception nine years ago, none could rival its popularity. In fact, it had become so much of an institution, it was almost respectable! Perhaps the personality of the owner had helped keep it to the forefront: certainly he actively courted publicity as he played out the fantasies of sexual liberation found between the pages of his magazine, with one highly publicised affair after another. And he did not always confine himself to one girl-friend at a time either. Often he had seven or eight living with him at his hilltop Bel Air mansion. Appropriately named 'The Harem', the interior was something straight out of the Arabian Nights, and as if there was any need to emphasise his main preoccupation, his swimming pool was built in the form of a naked woman!

Susan could not help but wonder at his choice of wife when the time came—if ever—for him to retire from the arena and settle down. Would this prize stud choose one of his luscious centrefolds as a mate? The image of a statuesque blonde flashed before her, walking down the aisle in the private chapel at Brocklehurst, naked, except for the Wentworth family diamonds! It was an amusing picture, but in view of his predilection for tasteless publicity, not an impossible one!

Yet if his adulthood had been a bed of roses and women, his childhood had been the opposite. His father, a surgeon, had been killed in the Korean war, leaving his widow with a trust fund for the private education of their four children, but very little other money to support them. She had returned to the medical studies she had forsaken on her marriage, and was now chief physician of a hospital in Phoenix. She had obviously had to sacrifice her time with her children in order to achieve this, and they had been brought up by a maiden aunt who still kept house for Gregg Saville's mother.

The detective had certainly done a thorough investigative job, and by the time Susan finished reading the file she felt she knew all she ever wanted to know about Gregg Saville, Don Juan of the 1980s.

She expressed that opinion later in the day to Jonathan Maddox, Stanley's partner and nephew. They were having dinner at a restaurant in Chelsea, a weekly habit she had tried to break, because she was not in love with him and did not wish to monopolise his time. But because he was convinced she would eventually agree to marry him, he persisted in his attentions. He was an attractive, intelligent companion, and they were never short of conversation, though they rarely discussed anything other than the office.

'Does that mean I won't have to worry about competing with Gregg Saville for your affections?' he asked with a smile.

'If he were the last man on earth, I'd become a misogamist!'

'That certainly makes you unique—but then I've known that for years.' He caught her hand in his big, warm one, and Susan wished with all her heart she loved him. Tall and tow-headed, with gentle brown eyes, he would make some girl an ideal husband.

'If this damned fraud case hadn't been put forward, I'd come to the States with you,' he told her.

'I couldn't see your uncle approving double expenses.'

'I'd have paid for my own trip. You're far too pretty to go abroad unchaperoned.' he said, his eyes openly admiring the delicate features, long, honey-blonde hair—drawn neatly back from her face into a soft coil at the nape of her neck and the slender, nicely rounded body, casually but fashionably attired in a green knit suit. All gave an aura of diffidence until one saw the stubbornness in the chin and determination in the eyes. They were her finest feature, he decided, being large and limpid, and the blue-green colour of the ocean. As she bent her head to sip her wine, a beam of light brought pale gold glints into the fair hair, and made him wonder if perhaps he was wrong, and this was her nicest feature. But then her mouth was delightful too: wide and generous, with a full lower-lip, while her skin was as delicate and pure as an English-rose. Mentally Jonathan gave himself a shake. He was eulogising her as if he were a lovesick teenager, not a man of thirty-five. What had happened to the hard-headed lawyer?

'You sound like my father,' Susan broke into his thoughts. 'He thinks the world's full of men without an honourable thought in their heads!'

'He's right—other than me, that is!'

'My Knight of the Round Table!' she teased.

'Sir Jonathan Galahad!' he quipped back.

'Then ask for a little wedge to be put under *this* table. It's wobbling.'

'At the price this restaurant charges they can bring us another,' he replied, testing it for himself.

'Don't make too much fuss or they might spit in my soup!' she protested.

'What?'

'That's what George Orwell said in *Down and Out in Paris and London.* He worked as a waiter when he was a young man, and according to him, if we knew half of what went on in the kitchens, we'd never eat again!'

'Well, if that's one way to get you up to my flat for a home-cooked meal, I shan't object!' he smiled.

'I worry about you,' she said seriously. 'You shouldn't be wasting your time on me.'

'It isn't a waste. You're the brainiest girl I know, and I enjoy your company.'

'Is that my main attraction to you?'

'Of course. That way, when we do marry, I can play golf all day, and you can go to the office!'

Susan laughed. 'I must say, when your uncle first took me on three years ago, I wondered if it was because of my friendship with the Duke and his family. But when he died, and I was still made a partner, I felt a whole lot better.'

'You were silly to have any doubts,' Jonathan assured her. 'If your degree hadn't been up to our requirements, we'd never have taken you on, even as a favour to a client as important as the Duke of Wentworth. You're an excellent lawyer, Susan—as well as being a beautiful girl. Your only drawback is that you refuse to marry me. But I'll still go on hoping.'

It was midnight by the time he left her at the door of her flat, which was on the top floor of a large Edwardian house in Belsize Park. It was a tiring climb up six flights of stairs, but the view from her windows made it worthwhile.

'I don't suppose you'll invite me in for a coffee?' he asked.

'You don't suppose right!'

'Don't blame me for trying.'

'I'd blame you if you didn't,' she smiled, and quickly closed the door on him.

In spite of the lateness of the hour, she did not feel tired, and decided a bath might help her to relax.

As she lay in the warm scented water, she reflected on the reasons for her edginess: sexual frustration. Twenty-five was too old an age to have reached without a love affair. She felt a need to be looked at with tenderness; to feel the sensuous pleasure of a man's touch, a man's hands on her body. But not Jonathan's, or any of the other men she knew. It was not because she did not find them attractive, it was simply that she could not accept the intimacy of a sexual relationship without love; and so far love had passed her by. Or it had since Charles.

As usual when she thought of him, it was with bitterness tinged with sadness. Sadness at his tragic death six months ago in a plane crash, when he was being ferried across the Channel to a race meeting in Deauville by a friend. And bitterness when she remembered his treatment of her, at the party she had given to celebrate her eighteenth birthday.

Charles was the nephew and heir of the Duke of Wentworth, and she had known him since he had come to live with his uncle as a boy of twelve, when his parents had been killed—ironically as things had turned out—in a light aircraft on the way to a holiday in the South of France. But then fact often had a habit of being stranger than fiction.

Susan had been born and raised in the village of Brocklehurst, where her father ran the local grocers shop. It was owned by the Duke—as was the rest of the village and about ten thousand acres of the surrounding countryside. He was an excellent landlord and took a personal interest in all his tenants and their families. Learning of Susan's desire to study law, he had written to his own solicitors requesting that she be articled to them upon completion of her studies at university.

'It's not an easy profession for a girl,' he had warned her, 'and the better the firm you are articled to, the better chance you have of being a success.'

But at eighteen, she had been more concerned with the present than the future, and particularly her future with Charles.

He had recently come down from Oxford, and was

attending an agricultural college in a nearby town. Since his return they had seen each other constantly, and her youthful crush had bloomed into first love. Charles seemed to feel the same, and in spite of the difference in their social standing, frequently took her out. Never once had she been made to feel out of place, even though her clothes were cheap, her jewellery strictly imitation, and her accent—until she had lost it at university—containing a definite country burr.

Yet though she had believed none of this mattered because they loved each other, Charles had been very conscious that it did, and on the night of her eighteenth birthday, as they wandered hand in hand in the garden of her parent's cottage, he had finally told her the truth.

'I think we should stop seeing each other, Susan,' he had announced quite suddenly. 'At least alone. People are beginning to talk.'

'Then let's get engaged,' she had replied, completely misunderstanding him. 'If it's my reputation you're worried about——'

'It's not yours,' he told her bluntly, 'it's mine. I've got to start thinking of the future—of settling down—I can't do that if my name's linked with yours. Don't look at me like that,' he said, seeing her expression. 'I never promised to marry you.'

'You said you loved me,' she had cried. 'Didn't you mean it?'

'I suppose I did at the time.' He had the good grace to look embarrassed. 'You're a lovely, sweet girl, and I'm very fond of you. But you're not . . . you're not . . .'

'One of *us*?' she had rounded on him furiously. 'Is that what you're too embarrassed to say?'

'All right, damn it, it is.' He turned to face her, his dark skin and hair robbed of colour by the moonlight.

It gave him a spineless quality she had never before noticed. Perhaps because she was really seeing him for the first time as a spineless snob. 'Saville's have always chosen the correct wives,' he went on, 'and I intend to do the same. I owe it to my heritage.'

'If the end result is you, I can't see any virtue in your heritage,' Susan had said coldly, and had run away from him, intent on putting as much distance between them as possible—although the cruelty of his words had already served to do that.

She had stormed into the house, and, oblivious of the curious stares of her parents and guests, had rushed up to her room. Falling on the bed in a paroxysm of tears, she had sobbed as if her heart would break and never mend.

But it had, of course, and looking back on her behaviour with the hindsight of maturity, she realised how childish and unsophisticated it had been.

Charles had not married for a couple of years—by which time his uncle had died and he became the tenth Duke—and because she was living away from home it was not difficult to avoid him, even on monthly visits to her parents. His wife Davina was the only daughter of a wealthy banker—who had ever heard of a poor one?—and blessed not only with the correct social standing for a Saville, but beauty too. It was only in the brains department that Susan felt she scored over her—but even there she was not too sure, for though the girl looked soft and feminine, with her limpid brown eyes and fluffy hair-style, she had a steam-roller's capacity for driving relentlessly over other people's wishes. It was a common gossip in the village that she was both master and mistress of Brocklehurst, and many blamed her for the tasteless additions to the house.

It had been open to the public for a number of years, but soon a maze, an amusement park, souvenir

shops and a hamburger restaurant were added.
Though Susan thought the ideas completely lacking
in taste, financially they had been a great success,
and Brocklehurst was soon third in the Stately
Home league—though still not completely paying its
way.

But now Charles was dead and the young Duchess
would have to move; not that there wasn't sufficient
space for her to live there even with Gregg Saville in
residence. With forty bedrooms to choose from, eight
reception rooms, a ballroom, billiards room, library
and servants' wing, they could avoid meeting each
other for months on end!

It was a relief to Susan to know it was not her
concern. Her dealings with the Savilles was virtually
over. Once she had seen the new Duke there would be
no further need to interest herself with their affairs.
The intricacies of the estate were too complex to be in
her charge, and were being handled by Stanley
Maddox.

As she draped her towel around her, she saw her
reflection in the mirror. With her long blonde hair
pinned roughly on top of her head, and her rounded
limbs, smooth and shiny from the water, she could
easily have passed for one of Gregg Saville's
centrefolds. A few more pounds on her slender frame
would not come amiss, though, she thought critically,
and straightened her shoulders. It made her breasts
tilt upwards provocatively. It was a pity no man had
seen her like this. Back to where I started half an hour
ago, she smiled to herself, and reached for her
nightdress.

A change of scene will do me good, she mused as
she climbed into bed. She would take advantage of her
week away and see the sights of Los Angeles—even if
it meant extending her stay by a few days. She was
sure Mr Maddox would not mind. Perhaps she might

even be able to consider marrying Jonathan. Was she expecting too much? she wondered. After all, once past the bedroom door, love might follow, instead of the other way round.

CHAPTER TWO

THE flight from Heathrow to Los Angeles was uneventful, though Susan, as usual, found it exhilarating to fly thirty thousand feet above the earth, with occasional glimpses of land and sea far below. But for the most part, when she was not eating the boring plastic food, or watching the even more boring plastic movie, she stared down at a blanket of cotton wool.

The plane was crowded and noisy, with several crying infants preventing sleep, and she looked with envy at the woman next to her when she produced a pair of earplugs, and almost immediately fell into a blissful slumber.

But when the great silver jet dipped its wings—as though paying homage to the fleecy white cloud that served to highlight the intense blue of the Californian sky—before it lowered its nose to the landing strip of Los Angeles airport, her flagging spirits revived. Peering through the window, she caught her first glimpse of the sprawling city—palm trees, swimming pools, lush greenery, skyscrapers and eight-lane freeways. Then the plane banked sharply and all she could see was brilliant blue sky.

Some fifteen minutes later Susan stepped out of the aircraft, the heat on her face unexpected after the cold, rainy summer's day she had left in London. It took an hour and a half to clear Immigration, though fortunately the air-conditioning kept bodies cool, even though several tempers grew hot. It never ceased to amaze her that American airports were so badly organised, when everything else ran so much more smoothly than their British counterparts. Past experience had taught her this when she had spent a working holiday as a camp counsellor on the East Coast during one of her long vacations.

It was nearly seven by the time she met Alvin Grant, the man from the detective agency. Imagining him as Humphrey Bogart playing the part of Phillip Marlowe with ill-fitting suit, loosely knotted tie and a cigarette dangling from the corner of his lips, she was surprised to find a tall, slim man in well cut slacks and jacket, with greying, closely cropped sandy hair.

Soon, her cases installed in the back of a small Honda—'Energy conservation,' he explained, seeing her surprise—they were driving towards the city. Although the sun had gone down, the air was still stifling, and the temperature well up in the eighties.

'Doesn't it cool down here at night?' she asked.

'Are you kidding?' he grinned. 'It was ninety-two earlier today. But don't worry, everywhere you go is air-conditioned, and you might even find you need something over your shoulders in some places, they turn it up so high.'

'Is it far to the hotel?' she asked.

'About twenty minutes. I suppose you're pretty tired?'

'I shan't say no to eight hours' sleep,' she smiled. 'I was too excited to get much last night.'

'Well, you'll have plenty of time to rest up.' He moved into the outside lane and made a left turn. 'I'm afraid I have some bad news for you. Mr Saville took off suddenly this morning for the desert, and he won't be returning for a few days.'

'I wish I'd known,' sighed Susan. 'I could have put off my flight.'

'His secretary only let *me* know this morning, and by then it was too late to do anything about it,' he explained. 'I did telephone Mr Maddox, though, and he said not to worry, but for you to go ahead and see the sights.'

'I'd prefer to get my business with Mr Saville over and done with before I relax,' she said. 'Is he incommunicado, or could I go out there and see him?'

'He's with his photographic team at a ghost town called Eureka. It's near Las Vegas. They're doing a session for the Christmas edition of *Playmate*, and they're camping out there too.'

'Camping out?' she looked surprised. 'I can't see Gregg Saville roughing it.'

'It's not that kind of camping,' Alvin smiled. 'They have their own trailers, with all modcons laid on.'

'Would it be possible for me to go out there?' she repeated.

'I don't see why not. You can drive it in four hours.'

'Then that's what I'll do. I'll hire a car as soon as I get to the hotel.'

For the next twenty minutes or so, the detective kept up a cheerful patter, pointing out things that might be of interest to her. But the drive was mainly through the suburbs, and the apartment blocks, ranch-style houses and modern shopping plazas all looked pretty much like their counterparts in any middle-class area of America. It was not until they entered Beverly Hills that Susan felt she had entered lotus land. Here, image threatened to overwhelm reality. Even the foliage was lusher, the streets more immaculate, pavements lined with close-cropped grass, and gardens luxuriant with exotic flowers, shrubs and trees. Each house was larger and more magnificent than its neighbour, and vied with it for individuality. There was a noticeable difference in the cars parked outside too; Cadillacs, Rolls-Royces, B.M.W.s and Mercedes, with a sprinkling of expensive English sports cars—perhaps for the younger generation or even the staff.

'Does Mr Saville live near here?' Susan asked.

'Just up the road in Bel Air. If you think these houses are something, you ain't seen nothin' yet!'

She smiled at his Al Jolson impersonation. 'If that's the case, he won't find Brocklehurst quite so overwhelming,' she said.

'You still can't compare it to one of your Stately Homes,' the detective commented. 'I'd love to be there when you tell him he's a duke. It's something straight out of fiction!'

'If you read it, you wouldn't believe it!' said Susan. 'But I must admit he's not the ideal heir.'

The man beside her chuckled. 'Nothing's perfect in this life—but at least he's young and good-looking, and fits the image. He could have been fat, bald and ugly.'

'I can see you're a man who likes to look on the bright side,' Susan observed. 'I'm afraid *my* profession has taught me the opposite. I only see the pitfalls.'

'I suppose I should too—after all, my job is allied to yours. But if I continually looked at the bad side of human nature, I'd get so depressed I'd change jobs.'

'Were you on the police force before?' she asked.

'How did you guess?'

'From the films,' she laughed. 'Private detectives always are.'

'Well, if you're a movie buff, you've certainly come to the right place.' He turned left again, and in a few minutes drew up under the portico of the Beverly Hilton Hotel. 'There's a gala evening on here, and lots of the stars are attending.'

'I doubt if I'll be able to keep awake—even to star-gaze!' She tried to control a yawn, but failed.

'You've a generous boss,' Alvin Grant commented, as he came round to open her door, before unlocking the boot for the bellboy to remove the luggage. 'This is one of our finest hotels.'

Loyalty forbade her telling him it had been a matter

of Hobson's choice. Other than a way-out motel, this was the only place that could accommodate her—and then only because of a last-minute cancellation.

The foyer, lit by a magnificent chandelier, was furnished opulently. It was busy, as were the expensive-looking shops opposite the reception desk.

'You're in the annexe,' she was informed by the efficient young desk clerk. 'It's just to the right of the main entrance, and has its own swimming pool. But of course the main pool is open to you, as are all our other amenities.'

He handed her a jumbo-size key, and she turned to Alvin. 'I'll go and freshen up, and then have something to eat. If you'd like to join me . . .'

'Thanks, but no, thanks!' he smiled. 'My wife is expecting me home for dinner. I'm sure you'd prefer to rest anyway. I'll call you in the morning to see what you're doing.'

This reminded her to see about hiring a car, which was easily and quickly accomplished, and by the time she reached her room on the second floor of the annexe, her luggage was already there, piled neatly on a webbed stool.

Pleasantly furnished in green and rose print, the room had two queen-sized beds, a small settee, a large colour T.V. set built into the wall opposite, and a mass of fitted cupboards. The bathroom was small but fully tiled, and contained an electric kettle with several sachets of tea, coffee, sugar and dried cream. She switched it on immediately, and while the water boiled started to unpack.

The view from her window wasn't great; it overlooked a busy side street, and she could hear cars swishing by in spite of the double glazing. But it was a pleasing and comforting sound, and somehow made her feel less alone. As did the television, which she switched on while eating her dinner.

After a while she could no longer keep her eyes open, and pushing the food trolley into the corridor, she locked her bedroom door, climbed into bed and fell immediately into a dreamless slumber.

The noise of the telephone awoke her, and she was not surprised to find it had gone eleven. She had slept for over twelve hours!

'I hope I didn't wake you?' It was Alvin Grant.

'Not at all,' Susan lied, trying to sound as bright and fresh as he did. 'I was just having a second cup of coffee in bed.' She went on to tell him she did not intend driving out to the desert until the following day. 'I thought I'd just relax around the pool and get some sun.'

'Well, you have my phone number,' he said. 'If you want me for anything, don't hesitate to call.'

What a kind man, she thought, as she made her way to the bathroom. If only he'd been the Duke of Wentworth's heir, how much more pleasant her task would have been!

She tried to put all thoughts of Gregg Saville out of her mind as she relaxed at the poolside under an umbrella. The sun was far too fierce to sit in for long, and although she tanned more easily than most blondes, she still had to be careful.

There were mainly children swimming in the pool; their parents apparently finding alcohol more cooling in the heat than water. Well, I'm an adult to, she smiled to herself, but I'll be a glutton, and have the best of both worlds. The service was quick and efficient, her Piña Colada delicious, and with a feeling of well-being, she made her way to the diving board at the far end.

Her progress was followed by every male over the age of fifteen, and the women eyed her too, but with envy, not lust! It made her conscious of how minimal her bikini was, the top cut low on her breasts and showing the violet shadow between them, while the brief pants were knotted in provocative bows on each side of her hips, breaking the long line from waist to thigh. With her long, silky blonde hair pulled back from her face into a ponytail, and no make-up except mascara—although there was little need to emphasise lashes that were already long enough to be taken for false—she looked far younger than her twenty-five years. She felt it too, today, perhaps exhilarated by the brilliant sunshine and glamorous surroundings. It would be all too easy to get used to an indolent life, she mused, as she swallow-dived into the sparkling water. Particularly here, with one sunlit day dissolving into another. How did one get any work done, with tennis, golf, the ocean and all the sports appertaining to it readily and cheaply available?

The hours passed all too quickly; a siesta in the shade on one of the comfortable loungers after a late and leisurely lunch, of lobster salad and a half bottle of excellent Californian Chablis, and then a repeat of the morning's programme: sun, swimming and long, cold drinks.

She changed for dinner, and debated whether to go out. But the idea of wandering around Los Angeles at night, alone, decided her in favour of the hotel.

She made her way to the main restaurant, only to find there was no à la carte, but a set menu, consisting of a cold and hot buffet. What decided her to stay was the fact that the room was nearly empty. She had been propositioned enough this afternoon to last her for some time, and it would be a relief to sit quietly, without being pestered. Whoever had said the American male was losing his libido because of female domination had obviously not visited California recently!

She did not linger over her meal; she intended to make an early start in the morning, although the girl at the Hertz desk and Alvin Grant had assured her it was an easy drive. She knew from past experience that it was easier to get into a city than out of it.

That, in fact, proved to be the case, in spite of the clearly written instructions that were handed to her together with the keys of her car. Hopelessly confused by underpasses, overpasses and interchanges, Susan found herself back on the same turn-off to the wrong freeway for the third time, and deciding it was better to ask the way to the San Bernadino Freeway than carry obstinately on in the hope that she would come across it by chance, she drew up behind a parked police car.

Contrary to popular rumour, she had not found American policemen to be either impolite or indifferent, and these two were no exception. They insisted on accompanying her, sirens blazing, as far as Claremont, where they assured her it was a straight route, and only fifteen minutes to the Interstate Highway.

Driving on the wrong side of the road held no particular terrors for her, as she had hired a car on her previous trip to the States, and she happily cruised along at fifty miles an hour in the fast lane, as there was little to admire by way of scenery, once the dark green alfalfa and the lusher greens of the citrus groves had given way to the dry desert scrublands. There were no golden, undulating sands of Arabia here, only sagebrush, tall saquery cacti—like giant candles pointing fingers to the brilliant cornflower blue sky— and undulating mountains in the distance, forming a hazy purple backdrop.

By the time she reached Barstow, she was ravenous, and turned into the first restaurant that took her fancy on the outskirts of the town. It was spotlessly clean and the service fast and professional. Her bacon was crisp, her eggs unbroken and grease-free, and the toast warm and flavoursome.

Deciding not to take any chances of losing her way again, when the young waitress came over with her bill she checked to make sure that her instructions were correct.

'Just keep going the same way as before,' the girl said, 'But if you're just going to see Eureka, you're wasting your time. I hear it's been hired out to *Playmate* magazine, and it's closed to the public for the next few days.' She gave a little giggle. 'You don't happen to be one of their models, do you?'

Flattered at the mistake—after all, whatever she thought of them, they were always quite luscious-looking—Susan shook her head.

'Didn't really think so,' the waitress continued, immediately dashing the pleasure she had felt. 'You're too small on top.' As if to illustrate her point, she thrust her own large, full breasts forward, so that she was almost bursting out of her gingham uniform.

'I have to meet someone connected with the magazine,' Susan murmured by way of an explanation.

'If you meet Mr Saville, perhaps you'll put in a good word for *me*. I'd just love to pose for him, and I hear he's recruiting some girls from Las Vegas.'

Promising to do so, Susan paid the bill. The heat on her face as she opened the door and stepped outside was like that of a blast-furnace. It had been bad enough in Los Angeles, but out here in the desert, the temperature was at least ten to fifteen degrees higher, and her green silk suit, that she had deemed suitable for a warm summer's day in London, felt uncomfortably hot and constricting.

The interior of her car did little to relieve her discomfort, as she had been unable to park in the shade, and the air-conditioning did not appear to be functioning at full blast. As she turned on to the Freeway again, she felt thoroughly disgruntled, her euphoria of the previous day completely gone. If she wanted to be perfectly honest with herself, her mood was not entirely due to the intensity of the heat. It was the dislike—no, distate—she felt for the task ahead of her. The very thought of Gregg Saville as heir to the Duke of Wentworth was anathema, and she admitted that as far as she was concerned, the usual impartiality she reserved for her clients had completely deserted her. But then why should she like him, when she knew enough about his private life not to? How *could* one have any regard for someone who made his living out of portraying women as sex objects, and refused, even in his personal life, to regard them as anything other than playmates? To him they were dolls, to be discarded when he became tired of them, which—if gossip columns were to be believed—rarely took longer than a couple of months. Here was a man of thirty-four, consistantly behaving like one of twenty-four.

Not for the first time Susan wondered if a man too immature to commit himself to one woman would be able to commit himself to the running of an estate as complex and demanding as Brocklehurst. Most likely he would sell it. True, several million pounds would have to be found to pay death duties, but they could be raised by the sale of the house and land. The offer from Sir William Royston would more than cover it, leaving sufficient for him never to work again for the rest of his life. But then he was probably in a position to do that already, she reminded herself.

A large sign loomed ahead of her—the turn-off for the ghost town.

At one time the old mining town had had a population of over ten thousand, but it had been deserted for more than seventy years before a private company had purchased it from the State of California, and in the early fifties had restored it as a tourist attraction. Fire and decay had destroyed most of it since the deposits of gold had run out, and the miners and their camp followers had quickly followed suit.

Seen from the distance, with its rough wooden buildings set on a sharp incline, the shaft of the mine at its feet, it gave one an eerie feeling of being transported back in time, and Susan would not have been surprised if a stagecoach with masked bandits at their heel had passed her by. But as she drew nearer, and the dry and dusty car park came into view, with the inevitable tumbleweed blowing across it in the hot desert wind, so did all the tell-tale trappings of modern civilisation: Coca-Cola, ice-cream and hot dog stands, souvenir stalls displaying their cheap tawdry wares at twice the price of the shops in the nearby town, and transistor radios blaring. Surprisingly, in view of the fact that Eureka was supposed to be closed to the public, they were doing a roaring trade, as was the car-park attendant, a friendly, fresh-faced college student, who explained why.

'They missed the notice just off the highway that says it's closed to the public, and they're making the most of what there is. I hear that takings have trebled since Mr Saville took this place over a couple of days ago.'

'It's a long way to come for a Coke and a hot dog,' Susan commented.

'Most people are just passers-by—tourists and such like who see the sign on the highway and think they'd like to take a look at the old town, so it's not as if they've come far out of their way.'

'I'm here to see Mr Saville,' she said. 'Where will I find him?'

'Up in the town,' he replied. 'But I hope you're expected. There are security guards on duty, and they're not the kind of guys you want to tangle with.'

His warning proved to be only too true, for as she reached the top of the incline that led to the main street, two burly men loomed menacingly in front of her, hands on the guns at the hips of their black uniforms.

'What do you want here?' the fairer of the two demanded sharply.

'I've come to see Mr Saville. I'm a model,' Susan improvised hurriedly, having no intention of telling these goons the real purpose of her visit.

They eyed her as if mentally undressing her, and fortunately seemed to like what they saw.

'I thought we'd seen the last of you,' the same man grunted. 'It's been like another gold rush!'

'You're English, aren't you?' his friend asked conversationally.

'The accent's a dead giveaway, isn't it?' she smiled.

'It's something you Limeys never seem to lose, however long you live here,' he remarked.

'I bet she's lost pretty well everything else,' the first one leered. 'How about a date later, gorgeous? I could show you a real good time.'

'Sorry, but I'm engaged, and my fiancé is very jealous.'

He was about to persist, but his friend threw him a warning look.

'Cut it out, Al,' he growled. 'Mr Saville's already warned you about chatting up the broads, and we don't want no more trouble—anyway, can't you see she's way out of your class?'

'Can you tell me how to find Mr Saville?' Susan took their disharmony as an opportunity to make her escape, and addressed herself to the nicer one of the two.

'In the saloon. It's up the hill to your right,' he instructed. 'You can't miss it.'

Following his directions, she passed the re-

constructed general stores, with goods displayed at
their original prices, a newspaper office, a Wells
Fargo depot, and the town jail. Even the sidewalks
were an exact replica of the old, consisting of plain
wooden planks, raised slightly from the ground to
allow for drainage. Only the horses were missing, tied
to the railings, but to compensate, she saw an
advertisement for a genuine Wild West shoot-out,
twice a day.

It was only a short walk to the fork in the road, but
the mid-afternoon sun beating down on her head made
it feel more like a couple of miles, and she licked her
dry lips and thought longingly of the Coca-Cola stand
she had derided just a few minutes ago. How
wonderful it would be to come across one now!

But as she rounded the corner, there was no sign of
a cold drink stand, for other than three large trailers
parked to one side, the street was deserted. In fact
there was no sign of life until she mounted the wooden
sidewalk and pushed open the slatted swing doors that
led into Miss Kitty's Saloon. Then the sight that met
her eyes made her gasp and recoil, and completely
forget about her thirst.

It could have been lifted from the set of a
Hollywood Western, so perfect was the reproduction
of decor and furnishings. Only the cast was different
from usual, for only one sex was represented.

Leaning against the brass railing of the rich,
mahogany bar were at least a dozen girls, posed in
such a way that their rear view was reflected in the
ornately gilded mirror behind. Dissimilar in height
and colouring, they were all pretty, slim, and shapely.
They had one other thing in common too; apart from
stetsons, gun-belts slung low on their hips, and
fringed cowboy boots, they were all stark naked!

But then so was the piano player, except for her
black garter belt, three-quarter-length black silk

stockings, high-heeled scarlet pumps, and matching ostrich plume falling from her elaborately coiffured hair to curl provocatively under her chin. With only slight variations—a flower here, a few paste diamonds placed strategically there—there were at least thirty more girls, either seated on the small stage, or round the tables playing cards or holding foaming beer mugs to their lips.

Embarrassment mingled with disgust kept Susan rooted to the spot. How could these girls allow themselves to be displayed like lumps of meat hanging in a butcher's shop? Didn't they find it debasing and distasteful, or were the rewards for having the most appealing flesh worth the indignity?

Such was her distaste that she barely noticed the other participants: photographers, their assistants, make-up girls, hairdressers putting a final touch to their creations, and a couple of secretaries taking notes. There were more than a dozen, all fully clothed, though, as was the man seated in the far corner, his long legs stretched out on the table in front of him as he half-tipped his chair back against the wall. He was talking to one of the models, and he was partly obscured by her, but from the way all attention seemed to be focused on him, she surmised this to be Gregg Saville.

'Hey, beautiful, come over and let me see you.'

The request came from the seated man, and unless she wanted to look like a fool, Susan had to answer it. Aware that all eyes were focused on her, she obeyed.

As she wended her way across the room, she saw that her guess had been correct. This *was* the man she had come to see. Dressed in blue jeans and matching sports shirt, he sported a plethora of gold chains around his powerful throat and wrists. Mutton dressed as lamb, she thought derisively, but had to admit he was even more handsome in the flesh than in his

picture. His hair was a darker blond than her own—
more bronze than honey—though a few strands at the
front were bleached fair by the sun. His skin was
tanned to almost the same shade, and was accentuated
by brilliant blue eyes. His sun-kissed colouring
lessened the patrician air of his precisely cut features,
and she was struck by the pure line of his long, narrow
nose, and wide, thin mouth, the top lip beautifully
curved.

'Mr Saville?' she asked, doing her best not to sound
as nervous as she felt. 'I'm Susan——'

'Well, Susie honey, we really have enough girls for
this scene,' he said, his bright blue eyes raking her
from head to toe. 'But get undressed and let me see if I
can use you on the stagecoach.'

'I'm afraid you don't understand. My name is
Susan——'

'Okay.' The voice, slow and melodius, mocked her.
'*Susan* honey, get undressed and let me see if I can use
you on the stagecoach—I'm sure you look even better
in the buff than you do now.'

There were several giggles, which only served to
add to her nervousness.

'I have no intention of getting undressed, Mr
Saville,' she answered, managing to sound calm, at
least to her own ears. 'And if you'd give me a chance
to finish speaking without interrupting, I'd tell you
why.'

'Do you think we could get on with shooting this?'
one of the men called out.

'Go ahead,' Gregg Saville instructed. 'It looks good
to me.' He turned his attention back to Susan. 'Now,
if you're shy and want a private viewing, I suggest you
come to my trailer.'

Said the spider to the fly, she thought, and would
love to have told him then and there that she was one
girl he had no hope of entangling in his web!

'I'm not shy,' she said instead.

'Then get undressed.'

'That's not what I'm here to do. I'm a lawyer, not a model, and I've come from England especially to see you.'

For a moment he stared at her then gave a slow smile that showed white teeth, which looked even whiter against the darkness of his skin. Was there nothing about this detestable man's looks that wasn't perfect?

'So you're a lawyer,' he commented. 'Tell me why you want to see me.'

'If the offer of your trailer still stands—with my clothes on—I'll tell you.'

Laconically he unfurled himself from his chair, six feet one of perfectly co-ordinated muscle and bone. Susan felt completely dwarfed by him, although above average height herself.

He murmured a few words to one of his aides—an attractive brunette in jeans and a halter top—and followed her outside.

The sound of country and Western music blared from the first trailer which, he told her, was the chuck wagon. It was a quaintly old-fashioned description, but there was nothing in the least old-fashioned about the gleaming equipment she glimpsed through the open door, nor the Chinese cook, in shorts and sweat-shirt, silently mouthing the words of the song as he rolled out some dough.

'He's my personal chef,' Gregg Saville explained, after he had stopped to speak to him. 'Although he was born in San Francisco, he trained in France, so I get the best of both worlds from his cooking.'

'It must be uncomfortable working in a confined space in this temperature,' she remarked.

'He likes it—says that when he works up a sweat, he also works up inspiration—he won't even use the air-conditioning in the kitchen at home.'

The middle trailer, which was also the largest of the three, was used as sleeping quarters for the crew, and they entered the last one. It was tastefully and expensively furnished, with brown suede-covered walls, lacquered furniture, creamy hide armchairs and settee, and eye-catching modern paintings, in vivid shades of green and yellow and peacock blue. It was also blissfully cool, and Susan could hear the faint hum of the air-conditioning.

'Take a seat,' Gregg Saville invited, 'while I pour the drinks. You will join me, I hope?'

'Yes—thank you. This is thirsty weather.'

'I'm having a Buck's Fizz,' he said. 'But if you'd care for something else——?'

A soft drink would have been more quenching, but because she felt tense, she decided to accept. The champagne might help to relax her.

'No, that's fine for me too.'

He opened the small fridge behind the bar, and took out a jug of orange juice and a bottle of Krug. Deftly popping the cork, he filled two glasses, then added a twist of fresh orange to the rim. As he handed her her drink, she noticed his long, lean fingers, the nails cut short and beautifully manicured. He probably has someone to shave him too, she thought disparagingly.

'You said you came here from England to see me.' His voice cut across her thoughts, as he seated himself on the cream leather settee opposite. 'Now, perhaps you'll explain why.'

Susan moistened her lips and leaned forward. 'As I've already told you, I'm a lawyer. My name is Susan Andrews, and I represent the firm of Maddox, Forbes and Maddox.'

'Never heard of them,' he commented. 'Should I have done?'

'They're your family's solicitors—and have been for the past forty years.'

'My family's solicitors?' he repeated, looking puzzled. 'You mean I have English relatives?'

'Didn't you know your great-great-grandparents originated from there?'

'Of course. But we always believed they were orphans and had no family. Are you sure I'm the man you want to see?'

'Quite sure, Mr Saville.' Placing her drink on one of the lacquered chests that served as a table, Susan opened her briefcase and extracted a batch of papers. 'These are the legal documents that prove beyond doubt that you are the sole heir to the title and estates of your late cousin, Charles Saville, tenth Duke of Wentworth.'

There was a short silence and a myriad expressions passed over his face.

'Did one of my friends put you up to this?' he demanded finally. 'Is it some kind of joke?'

'I know it sounds like one, but it isn't,' she insisted. Picking up the top few sheets of paper, and the photostat of Charles' death certificate, she placed them on the table in front of him. 'It won't take you very long to read these, and I'm sure they'll be enough to convince you I'm telling the truth.'

He stared at her for a moment, then leaned forward and took the pages.

'I hate refusing a pretty girl *anything*,' he said, and gave a slow smile. 'Even if it means making a complete fool of myself!'

The implication was that he still did not believe her, but to humour her was willing to play along. Fleetingly she wondered what she would do if he were still not convinced after examining the evidence. Return to Los Angeles, and approach *his* lawyer, was the obvious answer.

But her fears proved groundless, for after he had studied the documents, his good-humoured scepticism was replaced by genuine interest, and then, as he read the résumé of his family's history, total absorption. Throughout, he made no comment, and even when he had finished, did not speak.

'It seems apologies are in order,' he said finally, but his voice was ragged and uneven, as if he still had not recovered his equilibrium. 'Even a TV script-writer couldn't have dreamed up a scenario like this!'

'They say that truth is stranger than fiction.'

'I still can't take it in.' He touched his hand to his brow and massaged it gently with the tips of his fingers. 'You'll have to excuse me if I don't make much sense for a while.'

Susan nodded understandingly. 'At least you believe me. For a moment I thought I might have had a wasted journey.'

'A letter first would have made things a good deal easier for both of us,' he said, and there was implied criticism in his voice. 'This is one hell of a thing to spring on someone.'

'Mr Maddox realised it would be a shock either way, but thought it would simplify things to have me on the spot to answer any questions,' she explained.

He looked thoughtful for a moment, and then nodded, conceding her point. 'I can think of a few dozen already, so perhaps he was right. How long are you staying?'

'For as long as I'm needed.' She picked up the remaining batch of papers which contained a detailed report of the Saville family's assets and holdings, and placed them in front of him. 'I was going to suggest you go through this now, and then I could answer some of your more immediate questions before I return to Los Angeles. But if you'd rather I left it until you're feeling more composed . . .?'

He shook his head, and a thick strand fell forward. He brushed it back with an easy gesture, then riffled through the pages. 'It will take me some time to get through these. Would you care for another drink before I start, or some magazines?'

'Neither, thank you. But I wouldn't mind freshening up, if that's possible?'

'There's a shower-room through there,' he replied, indicating a door at the far end. 'Feel free to help yourself to anything you want—including the shower. There's warm as well as cold water.'

But 'through there', were two doors. One was probably a bedroom, she decided. But which? There was only one way to find out, and she turned the door handle to her right. There was a slight click, and as the velvet strains of Frank Sinatra singing 'I've Got You Under My Skin' wafted towards her, she realised the movement had activated a tape recorder. It activated the lights too, for simultaneously a king-size circular bed, on a raised, white-carpeted daïs, was softly illuminated by spotlights inset into the smoked mirrored ceiling. It was the only item of furniture in the room—but then what else would *he* need?—which measured about ten by ten, but because the walls were mirrored too, gave the illusion of being even larger. She also realised they were really vast cupboards, for one was slightly ajar, and gave her a glimpse of clothes within.

Black satin sheets and duvet covered the bed, and there was a matching quilted headboard, with so many gadgets inset into it that it looked like the flight-deck of Concorde!

The devil's lair, she reflected disdainfully, as she closed the door—though this particular man could truly be described as a lucky devil. For with all the qualifications to turn a girl's head—looks, charm, money, and a devil-may-care attitude—the sacrificial lambs did not have to be dragged to his altar, but came willingly!

The shower-room was completely mirrored too, but in an intricately faceted design that reflected many times over, and though small, was far from being purely functional, catering in particular for the sacrificial lamb brigade! Enormous fluffy monogrammed towels, half a dozen new toothbrushes—not everyone came prepared, it seemed—assorted gold-stoppered porcelain jars containing scented cotton-wool pads, body lotions, bath oils and talcum powder, a hair-dryer, and a pair of exquisite Lalique perfume atomisers, one of which Susan discovered was filled with Joy, her favourite scent.

Did one anoint oneself before or after? she debated. Most definitely after, she decided. Gregg Saville did not strike her as the sort of man who would need to have his senses titillated. Idly she wondered if he would proposition her, perhaps even suggest she spend the night here, rather than face the return journey to Los Angeles in the dark. How she would enjoy turning him down. Or would she? On a purely physical level there was no denying she found him attractive. But then, unless one was blind, senile or over eighty, it would be difficult not to! He was, after all, a gorgeous hunk of manhood.

Susan was startled by her thoughts. She had never considered herself susceptible to purely physical attributes, believing character far more important, and it was shattering to find she had been kidding herself. Another few glasses of champagne and it might be all too easy to look into those periwinkle-blue eyes and forget she despised him; except that she would end up despising *herself* even more in the morning.

CHAPTER THREE

WHEN Susan entered the living-room some twenty minutes later she found Gregg Saville still absorbed in the documents. Whatever her erotic thoughts about him, *he* hadn't had any towards her—yet.

'I haven't quite finished, I'm afraid,' he apologised, as she seated herself opposite him.

'Don't worry. Take as long as you need.' She reached for some magazines from the rack beneath the long table separating them.

'May I refresh your drink?' he asked. She noted he was no longer drinking champagne, but brandy. Understandably, he had felt the need for something stronger.

'No, thanks, I have to drive back to Los Angeles.'

'Some coffee, then? There's a percolator behind the bar.'

Well, he had not taken the opportunity to ask her to stay! But then, for the moment, his mind was occupied with more important thoughts.

'That would be lovely,' she answered. 'I'll help myself.'

She did so, and he continued with his reading. Idly she browsed through some *Architectural Digests*. But her interest in the homes of the rich and famous was lacklustre, even though the duplex apartment of Carter Kingman, her favourite interior designer, was one of the main features. It was difficult to concentrate her thoughts on anything other than the man opposite her.

She tried to visualise him as an English country gentleman, in tweeds and cap, striding through the mud in wellington boots, in the depths of winter. Consulting with Ted Swift, the bailiff; listening to the problems of his tenants, worrying about dry rot, peeling paper and paintwork, insurance, soaring fuel bills, and the hundred and one other problems that were part and parcel of running a great house and estate in these inflationary days. But her knowledge of him as a fun-loving playboy was far too vivid to let this more serious image impinge on it.

She had included some photographs of the house, the village and even the surrounding countryside, and she saw he was studying them now. He could not fail to be impressed by their beauty, but would he be moved by them too? Moved enough to stir his much-diluted Saville blood and raise within him something more than just a financial interest in his inheritance?

She did not have to wait long for an answer.

'I can see why my relatives were happy for Maddox, Forbes and Maddox to handle their affairs for the past forty years. They're not only extremely efficient, but thoughtful too,' he commented, indicating the photographs. 'I shall continue to retain them.'

'Thank you.'

He looked at her, an amused gleam in his eyes. 'On the contrary, it's *I* who should be thanking *you*! Had you not been so thorough, I would have remained plain Mr Saville for the rest of my days!'

'The idea of being a duke appeals to you, then?'

'In truth, I can't see myself using the title. Apart from the fact that I regard it as something of an anachronism, I'm far too American to feel comfortable with it.'

'Your blood's still part English,' Susan reminded him.

'But through generations of intermarriage, I'm afraid it's no longer blue!'

'That's all to the good. A red-blooded American is

just what's needed to renew the strain. The last couple of generations haven't been too prolific.'

'What about Fiona?' he asked, referring to Charles' sister. 'Hasn't she any children?'

'Two girls, but even if she has a boy, he can't inherit the title. That only comes through the male issue.'

'So if I die without having children, so does the family name?' She nodded, and he asked casually, 'How does she feel about a stranger inheriting the ancestral home and title?'

'I think she's relieved the line will continue,' Susan answered truthfully. 'Like all the Savilles, she has a great sense of history.'

'That's a very generous viewpoint, considering she would have inherited half the estate, had an heir not been found,' he commented.

'Fiona's husband is a property tycoon,' Susan replied. 'So if you're feeling guilty, you have no need. That goes for the Duchess too,' she added. 'Charles left her all his own personal money, and her father will probably leave her twice as much!'

'I wasn't feeling guilty,' he commented dryly, 'merely curious. I didn't imagine they'd be queueing for welfare.' His gaze rested on the photographs spread haphazardly on the table in front of him. 'From the looks of these, the house appears to be exceedingly well preserved.'

'To quote the estate agents, you could move in without spending a penny!'

'If all the bathrooms are as antiquated as this one, I can believe it!' he chuckled, pointing to one of the pictures. 'I'd guess at circa 1929!'

'Just be thankful they're not circa 1629! Inigo Jones may have been a master designer, but his plumbing left a lot to be desired!'

He smiled. 'Do you know the house well?'

'Yes. I was born in the village of Brocklehurst. My father runs the grocer's shop, and is one of the estate's tenants.'

'Is that why you were sent here, instead of one of the senior partners?' Her face flamed, and Gregg Saville looked perturbed. 'I didn't mean to imply that——'

'There's no need to apologise, she said stiffly. 'You're quite right. Normally something of this importance would have been handled by a senior partner. But it was thought my personal knowledge of the family and estate might be more useful to you than purely professional knowledge.'

He nodded understandingly, and then proceeding to put her to the test, asking several pertinent questions, and giving her instructions, which she jotted down in the notebook she had brought with her.

She was surprised at their depth, surprised too at his quick grasp of facts and figures. After all, he had only had time to skim through the documents appertaining to them.

'You've certainly proved your point,' he commended her finally. 'Perhaps when I visit Brocklehurst you'll give me the benefit of some more of your advice.'

'There's an extremely competent staff both in the house and on the estate,' she answered, intent on discouraging him. There was no way she was going to make herself available to him once she returned to England. 'Most of them have been with the family all their working lives, and they'll be of far more help than me.'

'All their working lives,' he repeated. 'That smacks of *Upstairs, Downstairs*.'

'In many ways country people still have those values,' she replied. 'Loyalty, honesty and respect are not dirty words to be laughed or sneered at.'

'And are *you* still a country girl at heart?'

'If you mean are those still my values, then the answer is yes.'

He gave her a slow, studied look. 'Are the rest of your values equally old-fashioned?'

From his tone, the innuendo was obvious. 'I left home at eighteen to go to university, Mr Saville. Does that answer your question?' she replied, cheeks pink, but manner cool. There was no way she was going to tell him the truth!

His wide mouth broke into a grin. 'I guess that means you no longer count as one of the village maidens—what a pity!'

'If you were reckoning on *that* particular privilege, I'll have to disillusion you. That old-fashioned we're not—though no doubt once it's known that *you're* the new lord of the manor, they'll be a few willing to accord you the favour!'

'You haven't informed the tenants and staff, then?'

'No, just the Duchess and Fiona. We didn't want the newspapers to get hold of the story of our search, and it would have been impossible for so many people to keep it a secret. If the news had leaked we'd have been flooded with false claims.'

'Well, there's no reason to keep it a secret any longer. As soon as my own lawyer has okayed everything, I'll get my P.R. man to arrange a press conference. I'd like you to share it with me. I think you deserve some of the limelight.'

'Thank you, but no,' said Susan firmly. 'Mr Maddox is against publicity for the firm.'

He looked surprised. 'Over here, that kind of publicity could bring in a million dollars' worth of extra business.'

'I doubt you'd have that drawing power in England,' she smiled. 'But I've no doubt we'd pick up a few new clients.'

'Do you share his point of view?'

'I'm a junior partner,' she prevaricated, 'and I do as I'm told.'

'That's a pity.' His eyes glinted. 'I'll need someone to fob off any awkward questions, and you're a far more tempting dish to set before the press than Gerry Rosen.' He named the man Susan knew to be his lawyer in Los Angeles.

'A glamorous figure like you has no need of a side-salad, Mr Saville—particularly when it comes fully dressed!'

'I see you haven't forgiven me for my mistake.' The glint in his eyes was more pronounced. 'But at least you know that if you ever want a change of scene, there's an opening for you on *Playmate*.'

His eyes rested on her, and she wished she did not find his look so disturbing.

'Not even a million pounds would tempt me to pose in the nude!' she said with asperity.

'If that were true, you'd be a most remarkable girl.'

'Money isn't everyone's Holy Grail, Mr Saville. And some people are more particular than others as to how they earn it.'

'The implication being that you don't approve of the way I earn mine?' he asked perceptively.

'Do *you*?' she continued.

He looked surprised by the question. 'Bright as well as beautiful,' he acknowledged.

'Thank you,' she smiled. 'But that doesn't answer my question.'

'I know. But then you didn't answer mine.'

'Do I need to state the obvious?'

His eyebrows moved slightly. 'Have you ever read *Playmate*?'

'Does anyone ever *read* it, Mr Saville?' she said cuttingly. 'I wasn't aware it was bought for its literary merits.'

'Two ex-presidents, and half a dozen Pulitzer Prize

winners would be disappointed to hear you say that.'
His voice was a low drawl. 'Not to mention several of
your own men of letters.'

'It takes more than a coating of gold to disguise
dross!'

She had got under his skin, if the flush coming into
it was anything to go by, but his reply, when it came,
showed no sign of anger, and she gave him full marks
for restraint.

'As a lawyer, surely your duty is to examine the
evidence before passing judgment?'

He leaned back against the cream leather cushions
and drew up a silk-socked ankle resting it on the knee
of his other leg in the posture of a man at ease with
himself both physically and mentally.

Susan envied him, wishing she felt equally relaxed.
But irritation with herself for speaking so bluntly
prevented it. She had regretted it immediately, but
there was no way of retracting. And of course his
criticism was just. Why in heaven's name hadn't she
thought to read his wretched magazine *first*, before
criticising it? Talking out of ignorance was no way to
win either his respect, or an argument, though why
she should care about the former, she did not stop to
think.

'You're quite right,' she conceded apologetically.
'But frankly, I'd be too embarrassed to buy a copy.'

'I'll have my secretary send one to your hotel.' He
waved her protest aside. 'I'd like you to see it,' he
insisted. 'Contrary to what you think, you'll find more
gold than dross!'

'Now you're so successful and can afford it, why
don't you go for pure gold?'

'Because then I wouldn't enjoy taking my work
home with me half so much!'

She could not think of a reply to this, and he saw it,
and laughed. It was a deep-throated sound and relaxed

his entire frame, making him look younger than his years.

'Poor Susan,' he mocked. 'How you wish I owned a magazine like *Time*, or *Geographical World*!'

Susan sipped her coffee, which was now cold, and did not answer, feeling she had already done enough to antagonise him.

'No comment?' he prompted softly. She shook her head and he half smiled. 'I suppose I've built a certain reputation, and like you, people are inclined to believe it without looking behind the image for the real man.'

'Perhaps if you worked less hard at promoting the image, they might take the man more seriously,' she suggested.

'No doubt you think I should sell my magazine and devote my life to preserving Brocklehurst?'

'Your family have cherished it for centuries. It would be nice to know their efforts haven't been wasted.'

'They did it out of a sense of duty,' he pointed out. 'As a stranger, I feel no such commitment.'

Susan thought of her parents, and all the other tenants on the estate. Many of them had relied on the patronage of the Savilles for generations. What would happen to them if the estate were sold and broken up? Sir William Royston's offer was a generous one, but someone less philanthropic might come along and offer even more.

'Naturally you're concerned for your parents,' Gregg Saville observed, cutting across her thoughts.

'If the estate were sold, they might be forced out,' she said frankly. 'They couldn't afford to pay an economical rent, and a stranger certainly wouldn't be prepared to subsidise them at their present one, as the late Duke and his uncle did. The other tenants are in the same position, of course,' she added.

'But surely they're protected by their leases?'

'Unfortunately they've never had them. The family didn't consider it necessary. They had a tradition of being fair landlords, and never envisaged a time when there would no longer be a Saville to carry on.'

'I appreciate what you say, but I have no particular desire to change my way of life. English country living is strictly for English country gentlemen with families.'

'Surely you'll marry some time or other?'

'Why should I play one instrument when I can have a whole orchestra?'

'You might fall in love,' Susan pointed out.

'If I can escape matrimony in California—where we have some of the most beautiful women in the world— I can escape it for ever,' he shrugged.

She wondered why he should want to. Perhaps he had had an unhappy love affair. But it was difficult to imagine any woman turning *him* down! No, most likely his attitude had been formed by the society in which he moved. However glamorous it appeared, it was not the most stable—one had only to look at the divorce rate to confirm that.

'I've seen too many marriages break up, leaving a train of unhappy, mixed-up kids,' he went on, exactly mirroring her thoughts. 'Staying single is the best way of guaranteeing it doesn't happen to me.'

'But fifty per cent of marriages still work,' she argued, quoting the latest American statistics. 'Yours might be one of them.'

'I prefer not to gamble on short odds! Besides, I have a low threshold of boredom. However lovely the face, after a few months, I need a change.'

'You make it sound as if beauty is your only criterion.'

'Mental stimulation I can get from my own sex!'

'Why? Don't you think women are your equal?'

'Of course I do—in their appropriate place.'

'Which, to you, means the kitchen or the bedroom!'

'Just the bedroom,' he grinned. 'Men are far more inventive in the kitchen!'

Susan knew he was teasing her; deliberately over-emphasising his point of view in order to put her in her place. But foolishly she rose to his baiting like a trout to a fly.

'With views like yours, it's not surprising the Women's Liberation movement tried to set fire to your offices,' she snapped, recalling the incident of a few months ago.

'I don't need to ask whether you'd have enjoyed watching the flames!'

'Any woman worth her salt would have been happy to light the match!' she answered tartly.

'None of *my* girl-friends would,' he stated. 'They know their place, and are happy to be kept there.'

'Perhaps if you mixed with *real* women, instead of the plastic variety, you'd form a different opinion.'

'Like you, for instance?'

He lifted his lids and gave her an intense stare. Even across the width of the table she felt the magnetic quality of it, and pressed her feet firmly on the ground, in order to keep them there.

'Other than as a client, you don't interest me in any way,' she replied.

'Don't I?' he asked, his ridiculously long lashes masking his eyes.

'No.' She searched for a way of proving it. 'I despise men who treat women purely as sex objects.'

'I suppose you want to be loved for your mind, not your body?'

'As well as, not only,' she corrected. 'Physical attraction is just as important as mental stimulation in a relationship.'

'But I don't have relationships—only love affairs.'

'Just affairs, Mr Saville. You don't know the meaning of love.'

He chuckled. 'You make a good sparring partner, Susan. You've boxed me into a corner.'

'I'm sure it won't be long before you come out fighting again!'

'You can bet on that. It takes more than a few sharp jabs to floor me!'

Susan lifted her hands and applauded him. 'Spoken like a true champion!'

'With such a beautiful opponent, the adrenalin soon starts flowing again!'

'One of us had better throw in the towel,' she smiled, 'or this could go on all night!'

'I have no objections to *that*.' His eyes, appraised her appreciatively. 'Though I can't promise to stick to verbal-games!'

She had left herself wide open to that one, and was annoyed with herself.

'I don't go in for casual sex, Mr Saville,' she said frostily.

'I promise you there's nothing casual about the way I make love!'

'I'm happy to take your word for that!' She reached for her briefcase and stood up. 'I don't think we have anything further to discuss, have we?'

His surprise at her rejection was so obvious, she had difficulty supressing a smile—but more of satisfaction than amusement.

'Are you engaged, or something?' he asked.

'No,' she replied, beginning to enjoy herself. 'And I haven't even got a boy-friend at the moment.' It was a lie, but one that Jonathan would no doubt approve of. 'You just don't turn me on, Mr Saville.'

His eyes glinted. 'That wasn't my impression.'

'You really believe you're irresistible, don't you?' she commented.

The glint in his eyes was more pronounced. 'I haven't had any evidence to the contrary.'

'Well, now you have, But with so many others clamouring for your favours, I'm sure your ego won't be too badly bruised.'

Their eyes met and held; hers green and defiant, his dark blue and . . . angry? or merely disappointed. It was difficult to say. But she noticed the colour had deepened to match his mood.

'I shall want my lawyers to go over these,' he said abruptly, motioning to the papers on the table in front of him. 'It will probably take a few days, though. Where can they reach you?'

'At the Beverly Hilton.' She gave him her extension number. 'I intend to do some sightseeing, but if they leave a message, I'll get back to them as soon as I can.'

'I'll let you know my intentions regarding Brocklehurst before you leave Los Angeles.' Lithely, he rose. 'Naturally, it's something I'll have to consider very carefully.'

Susan moved towards the door and he followed her. 'I'll walk you to your car,' he said politely.

'That's not necessary, thank you.' She turned round to face him. The movement brought them closer and he made no attempt to step away from her, but remained close, staring into her face. 'As it's still light, I thought I'd take the opportunity to wander round the town before I leave.'

He probably didn't believe her, and even more to the point couldn't have cared less. In his shoes, who could blame him?

He nodded curtly. 'Have a good journey back,' he said, and turned in the direction of the saloon.

Susan made her way towards her car with a sense of relief. Thank goodness that meeting was over. With a bit of luck, she would not have to see Gregg Saville again. He had certainly brought out the worst in her.

She had always thought herself tactful and controlled, yet this afternoon she had behaved both aggressively and provocatively—conduct that was unprofessional, to say the least.

Yet strangely, although ashamed of her behaviour, she felt no remorse. If anything, she felt a certain pride at having scored off him, cut him down to size. His look of surprise when she had turned him down was a memory to treasure. No client had ever elicited such varying emotions; no man, for that matter. But then she had never met anyone like Gregg Saville before.

And if this was what it did to her, pray heaven she never did again!

CHAPTER FOUR

IT was midnight by the time Susan arrived back in Los Angeles. In spite of her exhaustion, she telephoned her office in London, knowing they would be anxious to hear what had happened. It was only four o'clock in the afternoon in England, and Stanley Maddox and Jonathan were still in court, so she dictated a full account of her meeting with Gregg Saville to her senior partner's elderly but efficient secretary.

'Mr Saville wants me to keep myself available until his own lawyers have gone through everything,' Susan said finally. 'But I shall probably be able to return by the weekend.'

With her mind clear, she spent the next few days enjoying herself doing all the things tourists were expected to do: a half day at the Hollywood studios, seeing where the stars worked, then a bus tour of Beverly Hills and Bel Air to see where they lived; the Farmers' Market—a greengrocer to beat all greengrocers she had ever seen; Graumann's Chinese Theater, where she stood in the footprints of the famous; an evening concert at the Hollywood Bowl, Disneyland, and the equally makebelieve world of Rodeo Drive, the world's most expensive and exclusive shopping street.

It was here that temptation overcame her usual caution, and she splurged on a Ralph Lauren suit at one of the glossy boutiques. His cut was faultless, but as a flattering saleslady pointed out, so was Susan's figure, so why didn't she try a pair of matching slacks, and have an outfit that was multi-purpose?

With most of her five-hundred-pound bonus still intact—she had only bought a couple of summer dresses for her trip, and they had been in a sale—she did not need much persuading to add a matching blouse to her purchase; nor toning boots and a bag at Bonwit Teller, just a short walk away on Wilshire Boulevard.

Several presents later—inexpensive compared to most of Tiffany's prices, but rather more than she had ever spent before—she was dipping into her own money. But what the hell? She wouldn't be visiting Los Angeles again in a hurry, and her parents and friends would get a kick out of receiving gifts from the famous store.

With this in mind, she decided not to return to her hotel for her usual late swim, but to have a drink at the Beverly Wilshire, a few doors down. It was reputed to be one of the most glamorous hostelries in the world, and she was not disappointed. The entrance and lobby were like a movie set from the golden age of Hollywood; banks of flowers, ornately carved stonework, and the best in art-deco furnishings, while the stygian setting of the Padrino Bar was a perfect foil for the bright sunlight and heat outside.

Seating herself at a table in the corner, Susan glanced to left and right to make sure no one was watching her. Then gently she eased off her shoes, and with a sigh of sheer bliss wiggled her throbbing feet. Now she felt completely relaxed, and able to concentrate on making another of her big decisions of the day—what drink to order!

One of the nicest things about America, she reflected as she studied the cocktail list, was that a woman on her own was not treated as a second class citizen; a leper, to be shunted behind pillars or shown the worst tables at restaurants, and then ignored until all the men had been served.

Yet in spite of being treated as equals, they had not become masculine in the process; in general they were far more feminine than their English counterparts. They were not as sophisticated, though; in fact they were almost childish in their gullibility, as they slavishly embraced the latest media-promoted fads, be it exercise, art, clothes, books, plastic surgery, diet. . . . The list was endless, but concentrating on the latter, Susan could not suppress a smile. Not everyone adhered to the belief that thin was necessarily the most beautiful. She had seen some of the fattest women in her life while travelling in the States—more often than not, attired in figure-hugging crimplene pants suits—tucking into mounds of French fries, ice-cream and doughnuts, completely oblivious to their calorie value!

She helped herself to a handful of peanuts from the bowl in the centre of the table, and went on debating which kind of drink to order.

'Finding it difficult to make up your mind?' a male voice enquired in a friendly, well-educated drawl.

She regarded him coolly. Tall, lean, and well-dressed, he was also attractive, in spite of heavy-rimmed glasses. But she had no intention of encouraging his attentions.

'Not really,' she said matter-of-factly. 'I was thinking of something else, and not concentrating.'

'Then concentrate, and let *me* buy you a drink,' he smiled. It was a nice smile, and he knew it. 'You don't mind if I join you, do you?' The question was purely rhetorical, as he seated himself opposite her before she had a chance to answer. 'I don't make a habit of picking girls up in bars, if that's what you're thinking,' he said, reading her thoughts without difficulty. 'But I noticed you as you walked in, and there was something about you that interested me—other than your looks that is.'

It was about as original as 'haven't we met

somewhere before?' and Susan treated it with as much disdain. 'I'm afraid I can't reciprocate the compliment,' she said coldly.

'I wouldn't expect you to. Girls don't make passes at men who wear glasses!' The smile became dazzling as he turned the quote around. 'However, let me introduce myself. Carter Kingman, of Carter Kingman Associates. Perhaps you may know the name.'

Indeed she did, and now he had prompted her memory, the face too, for she had seen it only a few days ago in one of the *Architectural Digests* in Gregg Saville's trailer. He was one of America's foremost interior designers, and had been photographed in his own duplex.

'I do,' she admitted, 'and I very much admire your work. But I'd still prefer to buy my own drink, thank you.'

'I'm not discouraged,' he smiled again.

'Perhaps if I called the manager, you would be,' she said threateningly.

She was about to stand up when she remembered she was not wearing her shoes. She searched around the floor with her feet for them, but could find only one. Unless she wanted to disappear beneath the table and draw attention to her predicament, there was little she could do. Besides, Carter Kingman appeared quite unruffled by her threat.

'Please do,' he answered smoothly. 'He's a good friend of mine, and will vouch for me.' He gave her a long look. 'I'm not married, if that's what's worrying you?'

'But I *am*.' She grasped at this straw to be rid of him. 'And my husband's meeting me here.'

'You're a poor liar,' he chided gently, and looked at her hand. 'No ring, and you don't strike me as the liberated type who wouldn't wear one.'

'As we've only just met, I don't see how you can tell what type I am.'

'I know you're the type that appeals to me,' he smiled, 'and that's enough.'

'You're very persistent,' Susan said crossly.

He took this as acquiescence, and wasted no time in calling a waiter over. 'What will you have?'

'Champagne,' she replied promptly. Perhaps that would discourage him from picking up strange girls!

'Bring me a bottle of my usual, Mario,' he ordered, unperturbed.

He moved his chair slightly back, so that the wall light spilled over his features. They were craggy ones; a dominant nose, and a wide mouth with thin lips. His eyes, behind heavy black brows and equally dark-framed glasses, could not be clearly seen in this light, but there was a gleam in their depths that told Susan he was aware of her scrutiny, and she hastily looked away from them, up past his forehead, marked by two deep furrows, to the slightly receding black hair, the front and sides grey-flecked and cut aggressively short.

'Are you here on business or pleasure?' he asked conversationally. 'Or do you live in Los Angeles?'

'I live in England,' she answered shortly, 'and I'm here on business.'

'Are you alone in L.A.?'

'Yes.'

'May I ask what business you're in?'

'I'm a lawyer. I came here to see a client.'

He looked surprised. 'I hadn't figured you for a lawyer.'

Before she could learn what he had figured her for, the waiter arrived with a champagne bucket, a bottle of Dom Perignon nestling snugly in the crushed ice. Carter Kingman felt the neck with his hand, and then nodded. 'The temperature is perfect, Mario. You may pour it.'

'Are you staying at the hotel, Mr Kingman?' Susan

asked, when their glasses were filled, and the waiter had gone.

'The name is Carter,' he said, 'and yes, I am. I flew in from New York this morning, as it happens. We have an office in Los Angeles,' he explained, 'so I spend a few days a month here. I've often thought of buying an apartment, but they treat me so well at the hotel, I'm reluctant to move out. Running two homes can be a hassle anyway.'

'It's convenient for you too, I suppose. I noticed your offices opposite,' she said. 'I was admiring a pair of Tiffany lamps in the window earlier this afternoon, and wondering if they were real.'

'They are—that's why they aren't priced! But we do imitation ones as well.'

'They would be more suited to my pocket,' Susan smiled.

'Why not come across afterwards and take a look at them? I'll even give you a good discount.'

'Thank you, I may take you up on that.' There was no point in telling him she doubted if she could afford them even with a discount. He might think she was fishing for a present.

She sipped her champagne. It was delicious, and far nicer neat. That reminded her of Gregg Saville and the Buck's Fizz she had drunk with him. It was much nicer without him seated opposite her too, she thought inconsequentially.

'You've gone all cold on me again,' Carter Kingman remarked. 'Just when I thought you were beginning to defrost!'

'Sorry—I was thinking of my client,' she answered. 'He tends to have that effect on me.'

'I know the feeling,' he smiled sympathetically. 'I have clients like that too!'

In spite of her original misgivings at being picked up, she could not help warming to him.

'Do you have clients in England?' she asked.

'Only a few expatriates who still think that everything this side of the Atlantic has to be better.'

'And you don't agree?'

'I'd hate my rivals over there to hear me say it, but no. You have plenty of talent, without having to import it!'

'You're too modest,' she commented, liking him all the more for it. 'Whatever you say, we have no one of your stature.'

'You *really* are a fan, aren't you?' he said, looking pleased. 'Why not have dinner with me tonight, and then you can flatter me some more! And don't tell me you're busy,' he added quickly, 'because I won't believe you.'

'How about the proverbial headache? Would you believe that?'

He looked crestfallen. 'Don't tell me you *are* going to refuse?'

'No,' she laughed. 'I just don't want to appear too eager!'

He put his hand to his head in mock relief. 'Good. Where are you staying?'

'The Beverly Hilton.'

'Have you tried their l'Escoffier restaurant yet? It's one of the best in town.'

'So I've heard. But being on my own, I preferred to stick to places without dancing.'

'Don't you know anyone here?' Carter asked.

'Only my client, and I can't honestly say I *know* him.'

'If he hasn't asked you out, he must be happily married, over eighty, or blind!'

'None of those,' Susan laughed. 'Just a playboy who only likes his blondes dumb!'

'Which you obviously aren't,' he said complimentarily. 'Do you know, I don't even know your name.'

'It's Susan Andrews.'

'Well, Susan,' he said glancing at his watch, 'I had an appointment ten minutes ago in Bel Air.' He smiled and stood up. 'But I don't regret for a moment being late for it!'

'If it's with a client, I doubt if your sentiment will be shared!'

'This one won't mind when I tell him—he's a connoisseur of beautiful women himself.'

'Our clients should get together,' she commented. 'They have a lot in common, by the sound of it!'

He grinned. 'I'll pick you up at eight. Dress up if you like—as you haven't been dancing, I intend to rectify that.' He motioned to the champagne. 'And please feel free to finish the bottle. We've barely done it justice.'

She watched him as he crossed the room, stopping first to have a few words with the barman, before disappearing from view. She guessed his age to be in the mid-forties, rather older than any of the men she had dated previously. But like so many Americans, his manner was much younger. If he was as nice as he seemed, she was in for a pleasant evening; and if not— well, she still hadn't lost anything. She was tired of her own company, and whatever he had in mind for her *after* dinner, it would be a change not to spend the entire evening in almost total silence.

Deciding what to wear was no problem. She only had one dress with her that was suitable, and it was pure luck she had packed it. It had been in her mind that Gregg Saville might ask her out to dinner, as a matter of courtesy, but after their less than fond farewell on Monday, not surprisingly, she had heard nothing further from him. Nor his lawyers either, for that matter. If there was still no word from them tomorrow, she would telephone their office and find out what was happening.

But when she arrived back at her hotel, there was a message in her room, asking her to meet Gerry Rosen—Gregg Saville's lawyer—at ten o'clock next morning, but to telephone if she was unable to do so.

Although she had arranged to visit the J. Paul Getty Museum at Malibu in the morning, it was easily cancelled, and she lay on the bed and picked up the best-seller she had purchased at London Airport and had still not finished reading. But she found it impossible to concentrate properly, the words not making any sense as her eyelids grew heavier and heavier. The champagne was to blame, of course; she had had two more glasses after Carter Kingman had left her. She yawned and closed her eyes.

A noise like a car backfiring awoke her, but as she sat up she realised it was gunfire from the Western on television. She had switched it on automatically as soon as she entered the bedroom.

A couple of aspirins and a near-cold shower made her feel like new, and promptly at eight she was standing in the lobby waiting for Carter. Without conceit, she knew she looked her best. Apart from a faint application of blush-on to point up her cheekbones, she had not used any make-up; her skin was faintly tanned and it served as a foundation. The sun had lightened her hair, and tonight it was more gold than honey. She had loosened it from its usual chignon and it fell without a parting, softly to her shoulders, rippling like silk with the slightest movement of her head.

'You look good enough to eat—so you're lucky I'm on a diet!' the voice of Carter Kingman greeted her, and linking his arm through hers, he steered her outside to his car—a white Ferrari whose long, sleek body perfectly complimented the greyhound lines of his own.

'It's not mine,' he confided, as he set it in motion. 'I keep a Mercedes here, but believe it or not, it conked out in my client's driveway this afternoon. He offered me the loan of one of his, and I couldn't resist the chance to drive this little beauty.'

'*One* of his?' Susan queried with a smile. 'How many does he have?'

'Four. A Jaguar, a Cadillac, a BMW and this one.'

'He certainly believes in keeping his options open!' Susan quipped. 'The only countries missing are Japan and France.'

Carter chuckled. 'I didn't bother to mention the staff cars!'

'Was he annoyed with you for being late?'

'Not once I explained why. As I told you, he appreciates beautiful women.' He reached over and squeezed her hand. 'And you really are very lovely, Susan.'

'Thank you,' she murmured, and gently pulled her hand free. 'Where are we going?'

Unperturbed by her wish to keep the conversation neutral, he smiled, and put both hands back on the wheel.

'To The Bower. It's on the thirtieth floor of the Pan Pacific Airline Building, and has a fantastic view of the city.'

It was also the most beautiful restaurant Susan had ever been to—laid out as if it were a paved garden, each table set beneath a trellised bower of fresh flowers, their scents and variegated blossoms and colours a feast for both sight and senses. A floodlit fountain in the centre of the room, whose sliding glass roof was open to the warm night air, cascaded gently into a lily pond, while a mainly string orchestra played soft, appropriately romantic music.

'Would you like a drink in the bar first?' her companion asked.

'I think I'll remain teetotal tonight. I'm afraid I rather overdid the champagne after you left.'

That did not deter him from ordering another bottle when they were seated at one of the best tables by the windows.

'You're on holiday,' he pointed out, as the waiter filled her glass. 'So if you have a bit of a head in the morning, you can always lie in.'

'Not tomorrow, I'm afraid,' she told him. 'I have a business appointment in the morning.'

'But no arrangements for the evening, I hope, or the weekend?'

'I'm meeting the lawyer who represents my client's interests here,' she explained. 'And if all goes as I expect, I shall be leaving on Saturday or Sunday. It depends which day I can get a flight.'

'That's a pity. I thought we'd——'

She never did find out exactly what he had planned—perhaps it was as well—for before he could tell her, they were interrupted.

'Carter!' a male voice hailed cheerfully. 'What a lucky break finding you here!'

Susan did not need to turn her head to identify the intruder, for the timbre of his voice was unmistakable. But he had not had the same opportunity to recognise her, and as she looked round at him, and their eyes met, his widened perceptively.

'Well, well,' Gregg Saville murmured. 'So you're Carter's mysterious beauty. Now *that* really is a surprise!'

Susan smiled fleetingly. For some reason his presence put her immediately on edge.

'Hullo,' she said coolly. 'When did you get back?'

'Tuesday night. I decided to cut short my stay—for reasons I'm sure you understand.'

'You two *know* each other?' Carter looked bemused.

'Is there a pretty girl in L.A. I don't know?' Gregg

Saville's grin was wicked, tilting the corners of his mouth and giving him the look of a satyr.

'He's the client I came from England to see,' Susan explained, putting Carter out of his misery.

'Gregg honey, aren't you going to introduce *me*?'

The plaintive cry came from the exquisite, magnolia-skinned redhead at his side. Her voice had a strong Southern drawl, and was soft and sexy—cultivated, Susan suspected, to match her appearance.

He was immediately apologetic, and wasted no time in doing so. 'Susan Andrews, Carter Kingman—Honey Bunne,' he said briefly.

Carter gave a wide grin. 'Honey Bunne? You have to be kidding!'

'Can Ah help it if mah daddy had a strange sense of humour?' she pouted prettily.

'Let's hope he doesn't lose it when he sees you on the cover of next month's *Playmate*,' her companion smiled.

'There's nuthin' he can do about it, honey. Ah'm over eighteen.'

Not much over, I'll bet, Susan reflected, and catching Carter's eye, smiled. His expression told her he had had the same thought.

'Why don't we join you?' Gregg Saville suggested. 'It will be more fun than sitting separately.'

From the look on the faces of both Carter and Honey, his opinion was not shared. But he was oblivious of it, or pretended to be, and beckoned a waiter to draw up two chairs.

'So you're Susan's mystery client,' Carter said, after they were seated. 'I should have guessed it from what she told me about you.'

'I'm sure it wasn't very complimentary,' Gregg Saville smiled mockingly at her. 'Susan doesn't approve of me.'

'Well, I do, Gregg dahlin'.' Honey moved her chair

closer to prove it, joggling her breasts as she did so. They were large and full for someone so slim, and Susan noticed Carter eyeing them appreciatively.

'I'm relieved to know you're not completely irresistible,' Carter commented to Gregg, as the maitre d' presented them with the menus. 'It makes lesser mortals like myself, feel they're in with a chance!'

'I didn't say she didn't fancy me, just that she didn't like me,' Gregg Saville said slyly.

Susan felt an overwhelming urge to cut him down to size. He was so conceited, he had not believed she had meant what she said.

'Quite the contrary,' she said succinctly. 'I don't know you well enough not to *like* you.'

Carter glanced from one to the other. 'Shall we order?' he interjected tactfully.

'What do you recommend?' Susan asked, staring down at the outsize menus.

'Are you a meat or fish girl?'

'Meat, if it's the main course.'

'They do an excellent rack of lamb, with wine and herb stuffing.'

'It sounds delicious. But someone will have to share it with me. It's for two people.'

'I'm quite happy to,' Gregg Saville offered.

'If you don't mind. . . .'

'Mind?' Honey giggled. 'It's his favourite. He's always trying to talk me into having it.'

'Having *what*?' Carter asked innocently.

'Not *that*.' The girl giggled again. 'I never need persuading, do I, Gregg?'

'You have a remarkable appetite, my pet,' he drawled. 'Now stop being sexy, and think of your stomach.'

As soon as their orders had been taken, he stood up.

'How about a dance, Susan?' he asked casually. 'I'm

sure Carter won't mind giving Honey a turn around the floor.'

If he did, he was clever enough not to show it. After all, Gregg Saville was a client, first and foremost.

As they walked to the floor, Susan was aware her partner was the best-looking man in the restaurant; the best-looking man she had known, come to that. Small wonder women threw themselves at him. Small wonder he was conceited and arrogant too; that kind of worship would be enough to convert a saint to a sinner!

He was an excellent dancer, but then he was the sort of man who would want to excel at anything he did. Light on his feet, yet giving a suggestion of power, he guided her firmly, yet kept his hands gentle. So he would be as a lover, she mused; and was annoyed with herself for thinking of him in such intimate terms. Yet with the smell of his aftershave in her nostrils, and the touch of his smooth cheek against hers, it was difficult not to. She moved her head slightly, and her eyes met deep blue ones, the lids half-lowered, but not enough to hide their slumbrous gaze. His white linen suit was so fine it did not obliterate the steady beat of his heart, nor the steel-like quality of his thighs as they pressed ever closer.

Susan stiffened and pulled sharply away.

'What a pity,' he said huskily. 'I thought you were beginning to weaken.'

'You're not my type, Mr Saville.'

'But Carter is?'

'You sound disapproving,' she remarked.

'He's a three-time loser—or didn't you know?'

'You mean he's been to *prison*!'

He grinned. 'Let's say he received three life sentences, but didn't serve them!'

It took Susan a moment to grasp what he meant, but when she did, she could not help smiling. 'As it happens, he didn't mention that he was divorced. Just that he wasn't married.'

'That's true, at the moment, but from the way he raved about you, I suspect he fancies you for number four!'

'At least he's the marrying kind,' Susan pointed out.

'Is that the kind you prefer?'

'Yes.'

He whirled her around the floor before he spoke again. 'I thought you were a liberated female.'

'Because I believe in sexual equality, it doesn't mean I'm against marriage and the family.'

'So why aren't you married, then? You're intelligent and very lovely. What more could a man want?'

He made it sound an insult rather than a compliment, but she ignored it, and kept her temper.

'Perhaps it's because there are too many men like you around.'

'Don't you ever give a straight answer?' he asked irritably.

'I'm a lawyer, Mr Saville. What else do you expect?'

He threw back his head and laughed. It was an uninhibited sound, and several people turned their heads to look at him.

'I'd like to be a fly on the wall when you and Gerry get together,' he said, referring to his lawyer. 'He's a master of the art of prevarication.'

'I'm meeting him tomorrow, as you probably know.'

He nodded, but made no further comment. 'I have to admit you puzzle me, Susan,' he said instead. 'You refused *my* invitation, yet you allowed Carter to pick you up.'

'He's very persuasive—and I was tired of eating alone. Also, he didn't ask me to go to bed with him!'

'At least *I* was honest.' Gregg Saville's look was provocative. 'I'm sure that's what he has in mind for you *after* dinner.'

'Some men like the company of women other than for sex!' she said distantly.

'Sure they do. When it's their mother or their sisters!'

'You really are a chauvinist pig, aren't you?' she snapped.

'Most men are. But they haven't the guts to say so.'

'What makes *you* so brave?'

'My freedom. No one can tell me what to do or how to think.'

'You might not always be so pleased with your freedom. Today's Casanova is tomorrow's old roué.'

'I'd rather be an old roué than a henpecked husband,' he drawled.

'I'm sure you'd never be henpecked, Mr Saville.'

'Call me Gregg. It's much friendlier.'

'But I don't feel friendly towards you,' she answered coldly. 'I resent your intrusion this evening, and I'm sure Carter does as well. It's no coincidence that you came here, is it?'

'Of course not,' he admitted, unabashed. 'Carter told me about his mystery blonde, and when he refused to double date—which he'd never done before—I knew he'd found someone special. It made me curious, and I got my secretary to ring around until she found where he was taking you.'

'Don't you have any sense of loyalty where women are concerned?' Susan demanded. 'You're having a love affair with Honey, yet you came here this evening with the intention of dating Carter's girl if you fancied her!'

'My affair with Honey has nothing to do with love—as you so astutely pointed out the other day,' he reminded her. 'And vice versa,' he added, gesturing in Honey's direction.

Susan watched out of the corner of her eye. If the way Honey was dancing with Carter could be taken as vindication for his attitude, he was not lying. That was if you could call what they were doing dancing. It was more like making love standing up.

'Honey sells her favours to whomsoever can advance her career,' Gregg continued. 'For the moment that's me. If Carter were in the film business, she'd be ready to pack her bags and go to him tonight if he asked her.'

While she did not blame Gregg Saville for taking advantage of a girl like Honey, who used her body to get what she wanted, Susan was surprised he allowed himself to be exploited. The knowledge that he didn't care fuelled her general irritability into anger, though she was not sure whom it was directed against: Gregg Saville for being what he was, or herself for resenting it.

'Considering Carter can't help her, she isn't exactly giving him the cold-shoulder!' she commented.

'She's naïve enough to think it will make me jealous.' Gregg shrugged indifferently. 'Frankly, I'm not. She's good in bed, but no better than most.'

'Do you star-rate your girl-friends like hotels?' asked Susan caustically.

'On a grading of one to five!' he grinned cheekily. 'But if I could arouse *you* to a passion other than anger, I've a feeling you'd rate even higher!'

Susan felt herself redden, but Carter's intervention, as he drew level with them, saved her from replying.

'Our first course is on the table,' he said. 'I think we should sit down, or Susan's lobster bisque will get cold.'

During dinner, Carter monopolised the conversation, talking about his travels and some of his famous clients, in an interesting and amusing fashion. Gregg Saville had fallen strangely quiet and made little effort to join in. He even disappeared for twenty minutes towards the end of the meal, saying he had to make an urgent phone-call.

'Gregg dahlin', aren't you going to dance with me?' Honey pouted prettily at him as the coffee cups were being laid. 'They're playin' our song.'

'I know, sweetheart. I asked them to when I went to make my phone call.' He stubbed his cigar in an ashtray and stood up. 'Not that I needed an excuse to hold you close,' he added, his eyes moving languorously over her, before he led her on to the floor.

'He's a funny guy,' Carter murmured, as they followed them. 'Moody as hell, then charming as you like.'

'I think you've been a model of restraint,' said Susan. 'I don't know how you kept your temper when he turned up.'

'By thinking of business, sweetheart,' he confessed without embarrassment. 'He's got some big deal cooking in England—sounds like he's branching out into the hotel business, by the size of the job—and he wants me to handle the entire refurbishing.'

Brocklehurst, she thought. He must have decided to live there—or at least some of the time—if he intended to spend money on it.

'So it won't be goodbye tomorrow night, just au revoir,' Carter added with a smile, as he took her in his arms.

Comfortable in them—meaning, of course, that her sexuality did not feel threatened as it had when she was dancing with Gregg Saville—she gave herself up to the beat of the music, which had changed, as had the band, to Latin-American. Unlike her previous partner, Carter seemed content to hold her at arm's length, in both senses of the word, keeping his more intimate thoughts about her to himself, and performing a succession of intricate steps, which fortunately she had no difficulty in following. Perhaps he had decided the best way to handle her was by playing it cool. Certainly he was the perfect gentleman, even on the drive back to the hotel.

'I hope you didn't mind not going on with Gregg and Honey to that disco,' he said. 'I have to be up at seven.'

'I've had more than enough of them already.' She made no attempt to hide her feelings. 'Frankly, I'd much rather have spent the evening alone with you.'

'You've echoed my sentiments,' he answered, looking pleased. 'We'll do that tomorrow—and as it might be your last night here, I'll try to think up something special.'

'Why do you have to be up so early?' she asked curiously.

'I'm meeting my tennis partner at the Beverly Hills Country Club. It was the only time we could get a court.'

'You must love the game to get up that early,' she remarked.

'I never miss a day—even in New York. When the weather's bad I play indoors.'

His passion proved to be a good talking point, and they discussed the game and players until he drew up outside the Beverly Hilton.

'I'll see you up to your room,' he said, as he helped her out of the car.

'To the *door* of my room,' Susan corrected swiftly, but tempered her words with a smile.

'I never expected to go farther,' Carter assured her sincerely. 'I knew from the beginning you weren't a one-night-stand kind of gal.'

Which was more than could be said of their mutual client, Gregg Saville, she reflected wryly, after he had left her. What a swine that man was! Not content with his own conquests, he had tracked Carter down with the intention of muscling in on his. He had admitted it without so much as a qualm.

Even when he had discovered *she* was Carter's date,

it had not stopped him from flirting with her. There was a weakness in him that made him unable to accept rejection, and hers obviously piqued and puzzled him. He was too experienced not to realise that whatever she said to the contrary, she was not immune to him.

She wondered what his reaction would be if he knew she was still a virgin. Probably disbelief. Although she had told him she wished to marry, it would not occur to him that at twenty-five she had not yet had any love affairs.

But however much she was tempted, he was not the man to initiate her. There *had* to be more than passion to a relationship; not necessarily love, but at least affection or respect. And for a man like Gregg Saville, it would be impossible to feel either.

CHAPTER FIVE

THE offices of Smith, Rosen and Partners were in perfect keeping with the futuristic design of the building it was housed in, with glass and stainless steel predominating. Following the latest trend, Gerry Rosen was not seated behind a conventional desk, but a large table of moulded perspex.

He was a medium man; medium in size, height, looks and age. But mentally he was far from Joe Average. His mind was sharp as an electric saw, and almost as fast.

Of the points he wanted to discuss with her, none were of great importance, but they took time to explain and clarify, and it was nearly one o'clock by the time they had finished.

'There is something else I want to talk to you about,' he said, glancing at his watch. 'So why don't we kill two birds with one stone, and do it over lunch?'

They ate in a restaurant in the shopping plaza below, and over their chicken salad—served with a delicious Roquefort cheese dressing—they discussed their mutual client.

'There's going to be a hell of a lot of publicity when this story breaks,' Gerry commented. 'It's lucky Gregg is used to it, or he'd find it hard to handle.'

'When does he intend to announce it?'

'Tonight,' he answered, surprising her. 'On the Johnny Carson show. His mother and one of his sisters are flying in this afternoon from Phoenix to join him.'

'What about the other two?'

'They live here in Los Angeles. Not far from me, as it happens, in Brentwood.'

'It's a shame I'm going out tonight, I'd like to have seen his performance,' she commented.

'And knowing what a showman Gregg is, I'm sure that's what he'll give,' the other lawyer smiled. 'It's a pity so few people are allowed to see the real man.'

'Is there one? I get the impression he's lived with his image for so long, it's become a second skin.'

'If that were true, he wouldn't have decided to take a six month sabbatical from *Playmate* and go to England,' he said reprovingly. 'He took the points you made about Brocklehurst being part of your heritage, and the plight of its tenants, very seriously.'

'I can hardly believe his reasons are purely altruistic,' Susan scoffed.

'What other reasons could he possibly have?'

'An ego trip. He probably fancies himself as lord of the manor.'

'Gregg is too successful to need an ego trip,' Gerry argued.

On reflection, Susan had to admit he was probably right. She just did not want to credit him with any decent feelings.

'It's hardly a sacrifice for him to leave *Playmate*,' she argued obstinately, not wishing to openly admit she was wrong. 'If his publicity is to be believed, he spends more time playing than working.'

'I agree he doesn't live, breathe and sleep the magazine, as he used to, but he's still its guiding force, and controls every aspect of it.'

'He must have a competent staff after all these years, surely?'

'But no one can take Gregg's place. He's brilliant. He has a tremendous flair and feel for the business,' Gerry enthused with sincerity. 'Many people consider *Playmate* to be as good as *The New Yorker*.'

'If ever a comparison was invidious. . . .'

'Would you be surprised if I told you that almost as many women read *Playmate* as men?' he asked.

'Whatever turns you on, turns you on,' Susan shrugged.

'That's the whole point,' he said insistently. 'It's not predominantly a girlie magazine.'

'So Mr Saville assured me. But I haven't managed to buy a copy to find out.'

'There's a newsagent across the way. Let me treat you.'

'I doubt if they'll have any. I've tried several places and they're all sold out.'

'That must be because of Margo Mercer and Bob Nicholls,' he said, naming a famous Hollywood film actress and her equally famous husband. 'They were this month's centrefold.'

Susan pulled a face but made no comment. 'Mr Saville promised to send me a copy, but with so much on his mind, he's probably forgotten.'

'I doubt that. Gregg has a phenomenal memory. It can be very disconcerting at times.' He smiled, as if remembering an occasion.

'You seem to admire him tremendously,' she commented.

'I do, and not just because of his business accumen.'

'How long have you known him?'

'Ten years. I was dating his secretary. That's how we met.' Gerry waited while the waitress filled their coffee cups before continuing. 'As a matter of fact, I ended up marrying her.'

'At least it's a twist on the boss marrying his own secretary!'

'Luckily for me, Anne was immune to him. One of the few women who are,' the lawyer chuckled. 'Though I gather you aren't exactly a fan of his.'

'I'm not. Once I leave here, I shan't be seeing him

again. Mr Maddox will be handling his affairs in the future.'

'That's exactly what I wanted to talk to you about,' Gerry Rosen said. 'You'll be seeing a good deal of him for the next couple months. Last night he telephoned Mr Maddox and asked him to give you a leave of absence.'

'What?' she demanded. 'Why?'

'To act as his guide and mentor at Brocklehurst. You have personal knowledge of the estate, and Gregg was impressed enough by you to think you should continue to advise him.'

'There's a perfectly adequate staff to cope with any problems he might have.'

'He understands that, but there are certain important decisions he has to make, and any employee's advice is bound to be inhibited and biased to a degree.'

'How can he be sure mine won't be? After all, my parents are his tenants.'

'He trusts you enough to believe you won't let that influence you—and having spoken to you at some length myself, I agree with him.'

She was pleased by his comment. 'May I ask what these important decisions are?'

'Of course. He intends to ensure that the tenants' rights are protected in the event he should decide to dispose of the estate.'

Susan was surprised. 'You mean he's going to draw up leases?' she asked.

'More than that. He's prepared to sell the tenants their homes and farms should they prefer it, and he'd like you to act for them.'

'It's very unusual for the same solicitors to act for both parties,' she commented.

'But not illegal,' he stated correctly. The waitress appeared with some fresh coffee, and he waited until she had refilled their cups before continuing. 'It's not only the estate that concerns him, but his neighbours, and how best to get along with them. Your advice can be invaluable there too. They're bound to be rather different from the people he's used to.'

That was the understatement of the year, Susan thought wryly. They were of the ultra-conservative, huntin', shootin', fishin' variety, and would no doubt have equal difficulty reconciling themselves to the new owner of Brocklehurst. Nobody could possibly be a greater contrast to Charles. But they would not ignore Gregg, whatever their feelings. Indeed, they could not afford to. Apart from being the largest contributor to charity, espousing local causes in particular, the Savilles donated their home and grounds for a variety of events, including the main function of the winter season, the Hunt Ball. In fact, Master of the Hunt was one of the many titles the Duke of Wentworth automatically inherited. She only hoped the new Duke could ride. If not, he would have to take a crash course! In that part of the shires, a man was judged by two things; how well he sat a horse, and how well he held his liquor. She doubted Gregg Saville would need lessons for the latter!

'All he needs is a well-connected local girl to help him,' Susan said. 'And I'm sure the Duchess would be quite happy to find him someone.'

'It's not only a question of what he needs—with Gregg it never is,' Gerry interrupted gently. 'It's what he wants—and that appears to be you.'

'I'm a lawyer, not a nursemaid,' she snapped.

'And a very good one too, judging by today's performance,' he said smoothly.

But Susan refused to be deflected by compliments. 'Which is all the more reason for me to refuse. I have clients to consider.'

'But they could be handled by someone else, or Mr Maddox wouldn't have agreed to let you go,' he argued logically.

Susan could see she was making no headway with prevarication. The only recourse was to frankness.

'While I don't mind advising Mr Saville from London, I have no desire to work for him on a full-time basis,' she explained. 'I don't like him, and I have no intention of pretending I do.'

'I guessed you were going to say something like that, and I appreciate your frankness. So I'll be quite honest with you too. If you don't agree to do as he asks, he'll put Brocklehurst on the market immediately, and sell to the highest bidder.'

'But that's ridiculous, and unfair,' she protested angrily.

'Nevertheless that's what he says he'll do.'

'Perhaps if he knew my feelings——'

'I think he does—but it doesn't appear to bother him.'

'It's blackmail, pure and simple,' she stormed. 'He's taking advantage of me because of my parents.'

'All's fair in love and war.'

'The way I feel about your client, it can only mean war!'

Dark eyes, more amber than brown, regarded her. 'But you are going to surrender, nevertheless?'

'Never!' she declared vehemently. 'But being outflanked, for the moment I'll call a temporary truce.'

Gerry chuckled. 'I'd hate to be in Gregg's shoes when you decide to attack again!'

'Was he frightened to be in them today?' she asked scathingly. 'Is that why he isn't here?'

'One could call Gregg many things—and I've no doubt you would like to—but a coward isn't one of them.' He smiled again. 'He fully intended being here, as it happens, but he had a phone call from the studios asking him to attend a run-through of the show.'

'How soon will he be requiring my services?' she

asked, feeling somewhat deflated.

'Not until October some time. He has commitments until then.'

'And he won't visit, even for a few days, beforehand?'

'No. He decided a flying visit would be unsettling all round. Incidentally, Gregg wants you to stay at Brocklehurst—the house, I mean.'

'There's no need,' Susan said quickly. 'I'll stay with my parents.'

Gerry looked as if he was going to disagree, then thought better of it. He motioned the waitress for the bill, and there was a few minutes' silence while she wrote it out. 'I know you have a date for tonight,' he said. 'But if you're still here tomorrow evening, and are free, I'd like you to come over to the house for supper and meet Anne. We don't live far from Beverly Hills, and I'd be happy to pick you up.'

'That would be nice. Can I let you know later this afternoon?'

'There's no time limit,' he assured her. 'Even tomorrow will do. We're having a few friends over for a poolside barbecue, and my wife, bless her, always caters for at least ten extra!' He stood up. 'Can I give you a lift back to your hotel?'

'It's only a ten-minute walk,' she smiled, 'and the exercise will do me good. I've stuffed myself silly since I've been here.'

Watching her walk down the street, before turning into his office building, Gerry thought she had no need of exercise to keep her figure trim. Mint-julep cool in a pistachio silk suit, the thin material made her look even more slender than she was, emphasising the supple lines of her body. Luckily she was *not* as fragile or ethereal as she looked. Two months with Gregg at his most charming self would be enough to weaken the resolution of the strongest-minded girl, and he had a sneaking suspicion that was one of the objects of the exercise.

Although Gregg's reasons for wanting Susan to stay with him at Brocklehurst were bona fide, and made sense, his threat—that unless she compiled he would sell the estate—did not. His concern for the tenants was genuine, and would not be discarded so unthinkingly. And as for worrying about his neighbours, when Gerry had repeated *that* to Susan, he had found it difficult to keep a straight face. Gregg was the last person to worry about the mores of the English upper classes. They would have to fit in with him, rather than the other way around.

No, Susan had presented Gregg with a challenge to which he was totally unaccustomed: she had not succumbed. And instead of being put off by her rejection, it had only added spice to the chase, making him the more determined to seduce her. His decision to give the tenants their rights had presented him with the perfect opportunity to do so. He was ever one for combining business with pleasure if possible! Perhaps Susan had realised this. It would certainly account for her reluctance to accede to his wishes, even though it was in her parents' interest that she do so.

Susan admitted this to herself too, as she walked back to her hotel. She could not help but be grateful for Gregg Saville's largesse—brought about, she surmised, by guilt at his inheritance, but not to be denigrated, nevertheless. But it did not alter her opinion of him as a man, and she was determined not to let him add her to his collection of female scalps. But how to stop him? She was attracted to him and did not underrate his ability to wear her down. Perhaps accepting Jonathan's proposal might be the solution. But she dismissed that idea immediately. Apart from the fact that it would be unfair to him, Gregg Saville was *not* an English gentleman—if it came to that, he was not an American one either—and would have no compunction about poaching on another man's property.

Entering the foyer of the hotel, Susan was no nearer deciding what course of action to take, and concluded that like Scarlett O'Hara, she would think about it tomorrow. Why spoil her last day in Los Angeles?

By the time she had telephoned the airport, and had confirmation of a seat for a flight on the following day, it was too late to do any more sightseeing, so she headed for the pool, and whiled away the remainder of the afternoon swimming and sunbathing.

When Carter collected her, he was in high spirits. Gregg Saville had telephoned him earlier in the day to give him the news of his inheritance before it became public knowledge, and had also invited him to a party at his home later that evening, after his appearance on the Johnny Carson show.

'Naturally, he wants you to come along as well,' he said.

'I'm leaving tomorrow lunchtime, and I have to be up at the crack of dawn to get my hair done, and do some last-minute shopping,' she replied, not caring that the excuse sounded feeble, even to her own ears.

He looked as if he were about to comment, but then thought better of it, probably deciding the real reason for her refusal was none of his business.

'Well,' he smiled, 'it won't be starting till after twelve-thirty, so we've still got the whole evening ahead of us.'

His ebullience carried over to the following day, when he insisted on driving her to the airport, and regaling her with details of the most dazzling party of the year—of any year, for that matter—where it seemed champagne had flowed like water, and just about everyone who was anyone in showbiz had put in an appearance.

'You'll be flattered to know you were missed,' he smiled, as they drew up at the entrance to the airport building. 'Gregg seemed quite put out that you hadn't come with me.'

'No doubt he'll manage to live with his disappointment,' Susan said carelessly, and stepped out of the car.

She allowed Carter a kiss on the lips—it was the least she could do for all his trouble—and armed with the knowledge that she would be seeing a good deal more of him when he came over to England, made her way inside.

As predicted, the news had hit the headlines in all the media, and she bought three newspapers at the bookstand to take home with her, amused by their banner headlines.

'KING BECOMES DUKE,' ran one four-inch caption, and beneath: 'King of the girlie magazines, and international playboy, Gregg Saville, has become America's first Duke.'

But the second was her favourite. Headed, 'THE DUKE WORE JEANS,' it went on: 'It was announced last night on the Johnny Carson show, that Gregg Saville, owner of *Playmate* magazine, has inherited the ancient British title of Duke of Wentworth. Interviewing him at a celebration party at his Bel Air mansion, in the early hours of this morning, our reporter was disappointed to find that instead of traditional robes, the new duke wore jeans— Gucci belted and designer labelled, of course!'

The full story—giving Gregg's background, and that of the English branch of the family—with typical American efficiency they had managed to dig it up quickly—ran to several columns. And of course, they all featured pictures of the new Duke. His family too, arms around each other, staring somewhat dazedly into the camera. His sisters, who were attractive, resembled their mother, and were all married. One paper had even printed what each of their husbands did. Two worked for *Playmate*, while the third had no need to work at all. His father owned one of the largest hamburger chains in America.

Fortunately Susan's mind was given a rest from Gregg Saville for most of the journey, as her neighbour, a stringy weathered Texan, going to England to visit his married daughter, caught her eye and kept her engrossed with stories of oil prospecting.

In spite of the early hour—it was barely seven-thirty—Jonathan had come to meet her, and kissed her as if she had been gone for seven months instead of seven days.

'You look fantastic!' he enthused, carrying her luggage out to the car park. 'A tan suits you.'

'It suits everyone,' she smiled.

It was not until they were driving on the motorway that he questioned her about her visit, and he did not hide his disappointment when she told her about Carter.

'I don't have to tell you I haven't dated anyone else,' he said disconsolately.

'I wouldn't have minded if you had. I told you that before I left.' Susan covered his hand with her own, to soften the words. 'It was purely platonic, I assure you. He's not my type at all.'

'Nor is the handsome Mr Saville, from what you've told me.' His voice sounded relieved.

'Your uncle must have been surprised when he phoned to ask him to give me a leave of absence. I wonder he agreed.'

'Uncle Stanley may adopt a holier-than-thou attitude towards the practice, but he's a businessman at heart. We get a hefty retainer eacn year from the

Savilles, and there was no point in jeopardising it by refusing.'

Jonathan stopped at a delicatessen so that Susan could purchase some food and, though dropping with fatigue, she felt obliged to ask him up to her flat, to join her for breakfast.

It was nearly midday before he managed to tear himself away, and as soon as he left, she telephoned her parents.

They were delighted to learn she would be spending a couple of months at Brocklehurst, but staying with them presented a problem, for they now took in paying guests to supplement their income—flatly refusing to accept help from Susan—and had taken a booking for the two spare bedrooms, from a German teacher and his wife, who were on an exchange visit for six months.

'I'll write and put them off,' her mother suggested immediately.

'Of course not,' Susan replied. 'There's plenty of room at the house. I'll stay there.'

She had confided in her parents the reason for her trip to America, and as the Saturday papers had carried the story in full, everyone else at Brocklehurst now knew of it too. Naturally they were all agog to hear her impressions of the new Duke first hand. Promising to visit the following weekend, and satisfy everyone's curiosity, she rang off, and went to unpack.

Everything appeared to be going Gregg Saville's way, she mused, hanging up her dresses. If she hadn't known better she would have suspected him of planning it. She would put nothing past him. Now he would have her on the spot, morning, noon and night. It was the latter that made the urgency of finding a way to keep him at bay even more essential—unless, like the virgin about to be raped, she made up her mind to lie back and enjoy it!

She was still grappling with the problem when she climbed between the sheets. I'll have to take things as they come, she finally resigned herself, just before sleep overtook her. There was no point driving herself mad anticipating issues and trying to solve them, before they were presented to her. Perhaps she might even have misjudged his motives!

For the rest of the summer she did not hear anything directly from him, though a copy of *Playmate* was sent to her from the Beverly Hilton with a letter, explaining that they had placed the magazine in someone else's pigeon-hole by mistake, which was why she had not received it before she left.

It was from Stanley Maddox that she learned Gregg Saville would be arriving in England early in October, and spending a few days at the family-owned flat in Eaton Square, before going down to Brocklehurst. He had also inherited a villa at Cap Ferrat, in the South of France, and she wondered if he would be keeping it. When she voiced the question her senior partner told her that Mr Saville—no one could yet refer to him either as His Grace, or the Duke—would be staying there for the ten days prior to his visit to London.

'He's going to look the place over, and I gather he's thinking of developing some of the land. There's over ten acres, and it needs a small army of gardeners to care for it. It was never occupied for more than a couple of months a year, and the upkeep was always ridiculously out of proportion to its use.'

'Only if you haven't the money,' Susan observed dryly.

'All that glisters is not gold,' Mr Maddox chided. 'There are death duties to be paid, and most likely a hefty sum to satisfy the American tax authorities. It will run into millions, one way or another.'

'And probably take years to sort out,' Susan commented, thinking the accountants would grow rich in the meantime.

'Perhaps. But in the end, the money will still have to be found, and it's a painless way of raising it.'

It was certainly preferable to denuding the house of its treasures, as so many other Stately Home owners had been forced to do, and she was pleased Gregg had not contemplated this, but had looked for another way to raise the funds.

'By the way, Susan,' Stanley Maddox stopped her as she was about to leave the office, 'next time you visit your parents, the Duchess would like to see you.'

Susan wondered why. Perhaps, like everyone else at Brocklehurst, she wanted to question her about Gregg Saville. On the three occasions Susan had been home since returning from Los Angeles, she had been away visiting friends.

'As it happens, I'm going down on Saturday,' she said.

'Well, telephone and arrange to see her. She's a stickler for etiquette, and wouldn't like you just popping in.'

Susan knew this without being told. Davina's high-handed manner had made her thoroughly disliked.

The following Sunday morning, when Susan parked her Renault Four outside the imposing arched doorway of Brocklehurst, the weather was glorious. Not a cloud to be seen on the horizon, and the sun shining bright as a newly minted penny, instead of a pale autumnal gold.

As usual she felt as if she were seeing the Inigo Jones designed house for the first time, and as usual, it was neither the vastness of its spread, nor the huge rooms filled with priceless antiques and objets d'art, that filled her with awe. Rather it was the timelessness that impinged most deeply on her mind; the knowledge that long after she had gone, this great grey stone edifice, set beside a lazy chalky stream in the heart of the Cotswolds, would still remain.

Dawson, the butler, greeted her with a warm smile and ushered her into the great circular entrance hall, with its domed and moulded ceiling and inlaid marble floor. Hung with paintings by many famous artists, it led in turn to an endless number of rooms, a few of which functioned as offices for the staff. The first floor, reached by a cantilevered staircase, its wrought iron balustrade intricately worked into a pattern of trees and flowers that formed the letter S, led to the main reception rooms and bedrooms, some of which were still in use. As stately homes went, Brocklehurst was comparatively small, numbering only seventy-five rooms.

The Duchess was in the 'small' library, which was still about four times the size of the average drawing room, and at least twice as high. Panelled in Italian walnut, three walls were shelved, and filled with brightly jacketed leather-bound books. The fourth housed a television, the latest in video-cassette machines and a hi-fi.

However spring-like the weather outside, inside there was a definite chill to the air, and Susan wished she had taken her mother's advice and worn a heavy cardigan instead of a thin blazer. She shivered involuntarily, and the Duchess, seated in a pastel chintz wing chair, noticed.

'Sorry if it's a trifle cold in here,' she apologised. The voice was light and slightly breathless, with the curiously exaggerated vowels usually associated with exclusive boarding schools. 'But as I'm out for lunch and dinner, I told the maid not to bother to light a fire. How about a sherry to warm you up?'

It was not a drink Susan was partial to, but because her relationship with the Duchess was a formal one, she did not feel free to say so.

'That would be lovely,' she smiled, and Dawson immediately moved over to the drinks trolley in the far corner of the room.

'Do sit down,' Davina Wentworth instructed, indicating the settee opposite her.

Susan complied, and there was a short silence, while they waited for their drinks to be poured.

'I rarely touch alcohol,' the Duchess commented, as she took a glass of tonic water with a slice of lemon, from the silver salver. 'It's awfully bad for the skin.' Dark eyes ranged over Susan's face. 'Ageing, you know.'

The implication seemed to be that Susan's skin had aged so much already from excess that she was probably past caring, and once again she sensed the Duchess's dislike. It was the same whenever they met, and she had never been able to fathom the reason for it. Perhaps it was just the natural antipathy some pretty women felt in the presence of another. And Davina Wentworth was not merely pretty, but beautiful—jet black hair that silkily covered her skull and curled softly forward on either cheek, bright brown eyes with thick short lashes that marked them without softening them, and a small, full-lipped mouth. Her figure was a little too rounded, perhaps, but she had the height to carry it, and her legs were shapely.

'I won't keep you long,' she said, as soon as the butler had withdrawn.

'Don't worry, I have plenty of time,' said Susan.

'Actually, I only asked you to call out of idle curiosity,' she said, confirming Susan's suspicion. 'I wanted to get a first-hand impression of Mr Saville. One can never believe all one reads in the newspapers, can one?'

In this case one probably could, Susan thought to herself, but said aloud: 'He's good-looking—but then you know that from his photograph. Intelligent, a sense of humour, and an utter cad!'

Davina Wentworth looked amused by the summary. 'What a deliciously old-fashioned word to describe such a modern man!'

'The definition of a cad is one who lacks the instincts of a gentleman. I don't think Mr Saville would quarrel with it.'

'Gentlemanly instincts can be awfully boring,' the dark-haired girl commented. 'That's why so many women fall for cads.' The eyes were probing. 'I was wondering if you had, and that was the reason he'd asked you down here.'

Susan was furious that Davina should say such a thing, but managed to hide it. Nor would she say the purpose of her being here was to handle the contracts of the sale of the village properties to those who wanted to buy them. It was up to Gregg Saville to disclose this. Instead she said: 'Mr Saville thinks my knowledge of the estate will be useful to him, and also my knowledge of the social scene,' she explained.

'I can't see that he's right about either. Our estate manager knows more than you do about the running of this place, and as for the social scene. . . .' Thin black brows were raised questioningly. 'I think I'd be better qualified on that score, and I'd be more than happy to offer my services. After all, though you know everyone hereabouts, you could hardly call them your friends, as I can.'

There was no denying it was true. As a teenager, when she and Charles had been inseparable, Susan had mixed freely within his circle, but after they had split up, only Fiona, his sister, had continued to see her. Not that she had minded. She had her own friends, and had made many new ones at university.

'I shan't be moving out of here for some time yet,' Davina was speaking again. 'Perhaps three months or more. The builders have found dry rot in the house I've bought, and that's delayed everything.'

One of the instructions Gregg Saville had given Susan at their first meeting was to assure the Duchess that she was welcome to stay at Brocklehurst until her new home—a small manor some two miles away—was completed. But she did not think he had expected her to be there when he arrived to take over. Still, he was unlikely to object, and looking at it from her own point of view, it was the answer to a prayer. With Davina in residence here, she might not have to cope with his amorous advances.

'I'm perfectly agreeable,' Susan said, 'and I can't see why Mr Saville should object.'

'Good,' said Davina, swinging one leg over another. 'I'll start drawing up lists and planning parties—perhaps even an introductory ball. This house lends itself to entertaining on a grand scale.' Her eyes caressed the room, and then looked past Susan to the lawns sweeping up to the edge of the lake, and the woods beyond. 'You know, I fell in love with Brocklehurst the first time I was invited to stay here by Fiona, when we were at school together. Even as a young girl, I knew it was the perfect background for me.'

'You must feel sad at leaving,' Susan observed.

'Perhaps if things work out as I hope, I won't have to.'

There was no mistaking the implication, and Susan was so taken aback she spoke her thoughts aloud.

'You don't believe in wasting much time mourning the dead, do you?'

'Charles wouldn't want me to,' Davina Saville replied smoothly, not in the least put out by Susan's bluntness. 'He knew how I felt about Brocklehurst, and it was one of the reasons he married me. That, and the fact that our backgrounds were compatible.' She gave Susan the full battery of her eyes. 'But I was quite aware that he never really stopped loving you.'

Susan had often wondered if Charles had told his wife about herself, and the revelation that he had was a satisfactory explanation for her dislike. Even if Davina had not loved her husband, it would not stop her being jealous of another woman.

'Obviously Charles and I had a different conception of love,' Susan replied matter-of-factly, thankful the revelation had left her cold. The ghost of Charles had well and truly been laid to rest, as far as she was concerned.

'He had a tremendous sense of duty,' Davina said. 'That's something not many people can understand. And he would never marry out of his class.'

Susan could not help smiling. How silly such comments sounded today. Yet people of Davina's type still thought it.

'Didn't you mind marrying a man who still hankered for someone else?' she asked sweetly.

'Not at all. It was no hardship marrying Charles, any more than it will be marrying cousin Gregg,' Davina said in the same dulcet tones. 'Love does not have to be a requisite for the bedroom.'

Where have I heard *that* before? Susan thought dryly. It looked as if Gregg and Davina were made for each other!

'Hooking him might not be so easy,' Susan warned. 'He's a confirmed bachelor.'

'There's no such thing,' the girl opposite stated confidently. 'Men should be handled like horses—firmly but gently, but with a little something kept in reserve. It's an infallible recipe for breaking the most iron will!'

'Of a thoroughbred, perhaps,' Susan smiled, 'but not a bucking bronco!'

'As you've never been past the winning post, how would *you* know?'

Miaow, *miaow*! Susan had never thought of herself

as particularly catty, but this girl was having no difficulty ruffling her fur.

'Only because I've never been interested in hollow victories!' she found herself replying.

'Touché,' Davina Wentworth smiled, but gave the impression she was not amused. She stood up, indicating that their meeting was at an end. But not quite. As Susan moved towards the door she found her way barred by the other girl.

'Just so there's no misunderstanding, I assume you won't regard yourself as a guest, and that you'll find some way of occupying your evenings. You realise what I mean, don't you?'

'Perfectly,' Susan replied. 'As far as I'm concerned all the evenings are yours!'

CHAPTER SIX

FOR the next few weeks, Susan was kept busy with a particularly nasty and complicated divorce case, which she managed to win. But her feeling of euphoria was dampened by the news of Gregg Saville's arrival, a week earlier than expected.

'He's coming to the office tomorrow, at about twelve,' Stanley Maddox informed her.

'You won't need me, will you?' she asked, not wishing to see him any sooner than she had to.

'Not if you have something more pressing to do,' he replied.

She didn't, but instead of sending her junior to see the elderly widow who wanted to change her will for the umpteenth time, she went herself. She was obviously lonely, and glad to have someone to talk to, and it was nearly one-thirty before Susan found the heart to take leave.

Deciding to forgo lunch because of the lateness of the hour, she bought a container of coffee and a ham sandwich to eat in her office. There was no one at the switchboard, and she made a mental note to tick off the telephonist, then walked along the corridor and through her secretary's room. Her own door was slightly ajar and she noticed a mink coat draped on the chair opposite her desk. She was not expecting anyone and she wondered if a client had turned up unexpectedly.

'Sorry to have kept you,' she said breezily, 'but——' She stopped short, as Gregg Saville turned to greet her.

'I was beginning to think you'd taken the day off to

94

avoid seeing me,' he said tersely.

'I wasn't trying to avoid seeing you,' she snapped. 'I had an important appointment.'

'Oh yes?'

'Oh yes.'

All at once he smiled, his wide mouth curving at the edges, one well-shaped eyebrow raised teasingly. He was as casually dressed as when she had first seen him, except that his open-necked shirt had been replaced by a cream polo-necked cashmere, that showed every muscle of his broad chest and shoulders, and accentuated his sun-bronzed skin. If anything, he looked even more handsome than she remembered, and she moved across to stand behind her desk, glad to have it as a barrier between them.

'We seem to be turning two very small words into a quarrel,' he said. 'It's not the greatest introduction to a luncheon invitation.'

'If that's why you're here, you're wasting your time,' Susan answered coolly, indicating her sandwiches.

'I've booked a table for two at the Berkeley,' he said, 'and I won't take no for an answer.'

'Thank you, but I prefer a desk for *one* right here!'

'Come on, Susan,' he urged. 'You know you'd rather have lamb with herbs and Pouilly Fuissé than a dried-up ham sandwich and cold coffee. So why not give in gracefully, and agree?'

She tossed her head, and his smile widened. 'I promise to behave like a perfect English gentleman— in keeping with my new position!'

'I'm not dressed for the Berkeley,' she prevaricated, though she knew her red Carutti suit was more than suitable and he was dressed far more informally than herself anyway. 'I even wore an old coat today, because it was raining.'

'You look perfectly okay to me.' He moved forward

a few paces and let his glance travel over her. 'And there's no need to bother with a coat. My car's just across the road, and if you're cold, you can put mine round your shoulders.' He indicated the black glamma mink. 'It might be rather on the large side, though.'

For a moment she thought he was joking, but his expression told her he was not. Besides, who else could it belong to?

'You may behave like a perfect English gentleman,' she laughed, 'but you'll never look like one dressed in *that*!'

'What if I wear a bowler hat with it, and carry a rolled umbrella?'

The picture he conjured up was so ludicrous, she laughed again. 'I guess I'm just jealous, because I haven't got one!'

'If that's a hint, you'll have to do more than have lunch with me!' he grinned wickedly.

Once again Susan longed to hit him. Yet to show her annoyance would be playing right into his hands, and she decided it would be far more advantageous to pretend to play along with him.

'We've not stepped out of the office yet,' she said with a slight smile, 'and you're already breaking your promise!'

'Okay,' he chuckled. 'From now on, I shall only think pure thoughts!'

He gave her five minutes to repair her make-up—the restaurant closed at three, he explained, but they did not like to take orders after two-thirty—and when she reappeared from the cloakroom, he linked her arm in his and hurried her down the corridor towards the stairs. The building was coming back to life again as the staff returned from lunch, and as they reached the ground floor, they met her secretary.

'I left a note on your desk, Sandra,' Susan told her.

'I'm going out for lunch, and I'm not sure when I'll be back.'

But the girl was barely listening. Her attention was focused on the jean-clad man at Susan's side, who returned her worshipping gaze with a look of amusement.

'You're Gregg Sav—the Duke of Wentworth,' she corrected herself.

'Guilty as charged,' he answered solemnly.

'I—I read *Playmate*, every month, and I—I think it's absolutely wonderful,' she gulped.

'I don't suppose you share her point of view?' Gregg Saville asked, as he stopped at the doorway to ease himself into his coat.

Susan eyed him critically. It was a double-breasted affair, semi-fitted, and with a vent at the back. She had expected it to feminise him, but for some reason it had the opposite effect, the dark fur only serving to emphasise his masculinity.

'It's a good deal better than I'd expected,' she answered his question truthfully. 'I particularly enjoyed the current affairs review—it's very sharp and amusing—and that article about the cosmetic and cigarette industry's experiments with animals—did it reflect your own opinion?'

'Very much so,' he said emphatically. 'I'm a member of a group who've been lobbying the government for years to get more stringent laws passed. Ideally, of course, I'd like to see it stopped altogether.'

He took her arm again and shepherded her across the road to where a bottle green Rolls Corniche was parked on a double yellow line. Susan noticed a warden a few yards ahead, happily attaching a ticket to a battered-looking Datsun, but Gregg's car had been bypassed.

'I don't need to ask what you didn't like about my magazine!' he said, opening the door for her, and then walking round to the driving side. He set the car in motion, and as they passed the warden, he waved to her. 'She has a face like a battleaxe, but a heart of gold,' he remarked. 'I asked if I could leave my car here for a quarter of an hour, and she agreed like a lamb.'

'Perhaps she recognised the wolf in you!'

He chuckled. 'Or maybe she liked the car.'

'Is it yours?' Susan asked.

'No—it's on loan for a week from Jack Barclay's. They're hoping I'll like it enough to buy a new one.'

'And do you?'

'Yes—it drives like a dream. But I shan't make up my mind about it until I see how things go at Brocklehurst. I won't be short of wheels. Davina tells me there are several cars down there I can use, including her late husband's Aston Martin.'

'You've been in touch with the Duchess, then?'

'We spent the last week together at Cap Ferrat. She wrote to me, explaining that there was a delay in her leaving Brocklehurst, and when I phoned to tell her I was going to France, she asked if I'd like her to join me there.'

Well, she didn't waste much time putting her plan into action, Susan thought. 'I suppose you're kissing cousins now?'

Gregg took his eyes off road for a moment and gave her an amused look. 'If you mean are we sleeping together, why don't you just come straight out and ask it.'

'Would you tell me?'

'To my lawyer, my life is an open book!'

'Well, if the grin on your face is anything to go by, I don't need to ask if it had a happy ending!'

He chuckled. 'You do like to have the last word, don't you?'

'Only when I'm with you,' she replied coolly. 'You

seem to bring out the worst in me!'

He chuckled again, but did not reply, and the remainder of the journey passed in silence. Gregg drove well, dodging in and out of traffic and controlling the car with the same ease he displayed in his love life. So far, I'm one of the few he hasn't been able to control, Susan thought, and wondered if this would still be true two months hence.

'The Berkeley,' he said, as they drew up outside the cream stone hotel. 'And with five minutes to spare.'

Her door was immediately opened by an attendant, who smiled at Gregg Saville. 'Shall I park the Rolls for you, Mr Saville—or should I call you Your Grace?'

'Not if it means a bigger tip!' Gregg Saville grinned, and slapped the man lightly on the back.

'You obviously know him well,' Susan commented, as they entered the marble-halled foyer.

'I've stayed here ever since they rebuilt it,' he answered. 'And I shall probably go on doing so after this trip. The flat is enormous, and quite ridiculous for one person.'

Things had not gone Davina's way just yet, Susan mused. But then the girl had not yet been seen in her best setting. She fitted into Brocklehurst like a jewel into a crown, and if Gregg Saville did decide to keep the estate and live there, even part of the time, he might also decide he needed a consort capable of running it. And whatever his assertion to the contrary, Susan was inclined to agree with Davina's premise that there was no such thing as a confirmed bachelor. Given the correct impetus, even the mighty could fall. The important thing was to be on hand to catch him!

'It's a pity we haven't time for a drink in the bar first,' the man in her thoughts said, as he led her through the beautifully panelled sitting room with its crystal chandelier, to the spacious but extremely pretty restaurant. 'It's one of the most comfortable in London, and they make the best Bloody Mary outside New York.'

It was obvious he was well known here too, from the way the maitre d' rushed forward to greet him, and the waiters buzzed around, before discreetly leaving them to make their own choice of food.

In spite of the lateness of the hour, the room was still fairly full, most of the diners being men. All were conservatively dressed and Gregg Saville stuck out like a sore thumb. But it was not just his clothes that marked him as different, but his looks—which outshone every other man in the room—and manner. He displayed none of the polite unconscious—and sometimes not so unconscious—imperiousness of the rich, when addressing the people who served him, and spoke to the head waiter and commis boys in an easy, friendly manner, without being in the least condescending.

By the time they reached the coffee stage Susan was feeling totally relaxed. As well she should after finishing the half bottle of hock Gregg had insisted on ordering for her when he remembered she did not like red wine. They had talked on a wide range of topics, ranging from old movies, politics—his were as liberal as her own—and mild gossip about his many famous friends, to their mutual liking for cream with everything, and large dogs.

'I have a red setter at home,' he told her, 'and one of the reasons I could never live here for long stretches at a time is because she pines for me. In fact she pines so much I'm on the lookout for another bitch as a companion.'

'You could bring her with you,' Susan suggested.

'But then she would have to be in quarantine for six months,' he pointed out. 'That would only be sensible if I were to live here permanently.'

'You might even change your mind and do that, once you've seen the house.'

'You're obviously expecting it to be love at first sight,' he half smiled. 'But remember, I'm not the sort who loses his head easily.'

A waiter appeared with a plate of petits fours, and Susan helped herself to a pink frosted Cape gooseberry.

'For someone so slim, you have an extraordinarily healthy appetite,' he remarked with a smile.

'I do enjoy eating,' she conceded, 'and luckily I have no weight problem.'

'No other problem either, I'll bet. From what you've said, you strike me as leading a very uncomplicated life.'

She bit back a sigh. Yet until the advent of this man in her life it *had* been uncomplicated. And once the next two months were over, it would be again, she supposed. But at this moment, sitting so close she could feel the warmth that emenated from him, and see the individual lashes that marked those piercing, devil-may-care eyes, it seemed a long way away.

'I suppose I have been lucky,' she admitted, 'and the best part was having such super parents. I've always been able to talk to them about everything, and though it stretched their finances when I told them I wanted to go to university and read law, they never allowed me to realise how much of a struggle it was for them. Young people only see what they want to see,' she remarked, 'otherwise I'd have realised it for myself.'

'Do they just rely on trade from the other villagers and the estate's workers?' Gregg asked with interest.

'In the summer, when the house is open to the public, we have quite a number of tourists, and since Charles married, and the Duchess added the fair-ground, café and maze, that trade has increased considerably. So they're a lot better off financially than they were when I was studying.'

'Yes,' he said thoughtfully, 'Davina seems to have done quite a good job there—though it strikes me as being a bit of a three-ring circus.'

'I agree. But it's impossible to attract the crowds to a Stately Home, however beautiful, merely because of its historical interest. There are too many others with the same claim.'

He nodded understandingly, and then, because the mood of intimacy was still upon her, Susan posed a personal question to him.

'What was your childhood like?'

'Good,' he said succinctly. 'Not as ideal as yours perhaps, bearing in mind that my father was killed when I was small. But I was fortunate my mother had a brother living nearby, and he treated my sisters and myself as if we were his own.'

'And your mother? What's she like?'

A tender look passed over his face. 'She's an idealist. She could have gone into private practice and made a fortune, but she preferred to stay at the hospital where she studied. She's had her just reward, of course,' he added with obvious pride. 'She's now head physician. Not bad going for a woman, when you consider there's still so much prejudice within the medical profession.

'Not just the medical profession,' Susan pointed out forcefully. 'There's prejudice against women wherever they have to compete with men.'

· 'But in some cases, it's justified,' Gregg argued. 'Women do tend to give up their careers and jobs when they marry and have children, and if an employer is thinking of the future, and the time and money that often has to be expended on training ... Well, one can't always criticise them for choosing a man.'

'I'd like to believe that was the reason,' Susan said. 'But in the main, men don't like to think that women are as capable of doing their jobs as they are. They see it as a challenge to their manhood.'

'Women may be as capable, but because their make-up is different their approach and interpretation is different too.'

'I agree. But as long as we do our job as well, I can't see that anything else matters. I only wish we'd had more say in world affairs over the past few hundred years—I'm damn sure we wouldn't have made as much of a mess of things as you have. We may be illogical at times and even emotional, but we're far more practical.'

'They say that behind every great man lies a woman,' Gregg grinned. 'Perhaps they were all henpecked, and doing as their womenfolk told them!'

'That's certainly a novel way of getting off the hook,' she smiled.

'What would you expect from a slippery customer like me!'

He beckoned the waiter for the bill, and while they waited, Susan asked him how Carter was, and if he had seen anything of him.

A scowl marked his good-looking face, yet it only served to make him look even more handsome. 'Are you making conversation, or do you really care?'

'When I have nothing to say, I usually remain silent,' she answered waspishly, wondering why he should look so put out by her question.

'Sorry,' he replied, not bothering to look it. 'Carter's fine. He'll be over here next month. I have a few ideas for the house, and I want to see if they're viable.'

'I'll look forward to seeing him,' Susan enthused, deciding it might not be a bad idea to encourage the belief that she had more than a passing interest in Carter. 'We had a great time.'

'We could have had an even better one,' Gregg said softly.

'Except that I didn't like the kind of time *you* were offering!'

He relaxed against his chair. 'Well, as you can see, I'm a reformed character now.'

'A leopard doesn't change its spots!'

'There's a first time for everything.'

'If you say so, Mr Saville.'

'For heaven's sake stop calling me *Mr* Saville,' he said irritably. 'The name is Gregg.'

He rose, as the waiter returned with his credit card and receipt. 'Are you going back to your office, or going home?' he asked, glancing down at the gold Rolex watch at his wrist. 'It's nearly four-thirty.'

'I don't feel like going back to the office,' Susan admitted, 'but I'm afraid I have to. I can get a taxi, though. I'm sure it's out of your way.'

'I brought you here, and I'll take you back,' he insisted, and led her out to the car, parked in the bay just outside the entrance.

'I shall be going down to Brocklehurst on Tuesday,' he said as they set off. 'I thought perhaps it might be a good idea if you came with me, and gave me a lift in your car.'

'Very well.'

'I'm relieved *that's* settled without argument!'

For the next few minutes he concentrated on the road, negotiating Hyde Park Corner, and manoeuvring into the right lane of traffic to turn into the park itself.

'Did Mr Maddox tell you the purpose of my trip to France?' he asked, as they picked up speed again.

'He said you wanted to develop the land at Cap Ferrat.'

'Right, and it looks like coming off—with most of

the profits kept in the family. I have you to thank for it,' he added.

'Really?'

'Yes. You were the one who told me Charles' brother-in-law was in the property business.'

'You mean you're going into partnership with Fiona's husband?'

He nodded. 'I wrote to him from Los Angeles to see if the venture would interest him, and it did. He invited me to spend a few days with himself and Fiona at their château to discuss it further, and then flew with me down to Nice.'

'That was very enterprising of you,' Susan commented.

'It seemed the obvious thing to do once the idea of developing the land had taken shape. Louis is quite a guy, incidentally, and Fiona's great too. She's a down-to-earth kind of girl, with none of the pretensions of the French aristocracy, and none of the class snobbery of the British either. She sends her love, by the way, and wants to know when you're going to keep your promise to visit her.'

'Perhaps in the spring,' Susan answered. 'But that's what I always say!'

'Don't you keep your word?'

'I try, but I wasn't sure how I'd fit in to French social life.'

'You'd fit in anywhere.'

The look in his eyes as he gave her a swift glance made it clear where he particularly felt she would fit, and Susan's cheeks burned. With relief she saw they were nearing the office, and as soon as he drew the car to a stop, she jumped out.

'You won't always escape me,' Gregg told her. 'I'll phone you Monday night and arrange a time for you to collect me.'

'Fine. Thank you for a lovely lunch.'

'I hope it will be the first of many.'

Knowing it would be, and also knowing how dangerous it could be for her peace of mind, Susan retired to her office. She was vaguely surprised he had not asked to see her over the weekend—put out by it, if she were honest—and wondered whether he was seeing Davina in town, or some other woman. What a silly question! There could always be other women in his life. He was that sort of man.

CHAPTER SEVEN

On Saturday Susan went with Jonathan to Ken Lo's in Ebury Street. It was her favourite Chinese restaurant, and she happily ate her way through the menu; fried seaweed, shark's fin soup, Peking duck, sesame prawns, pancake rolls, and fried pineapple balls.

Afterwards he took her to a disco, where they danced until two o'clock, and though she yawned several times in the car, he rufused to take the hint, and asked if he could come up for a nightcap.

She knew what that meant, and though she did not find his lovemaking unpleasant, it did not excite her to any degree either.

He put his arms around her as soon as they entered the living-room, but as his kiss deepened, and his hands went to curve her breasts, instead of responding, she became irritatingly aware of everything around her; the crackle of water in the radiator pipes as they cooled, the bark of a dog in the distance, and a coffee stain on the nest of tables. This was even worse than usual.

He started to undo the tiny buttons at the front of her dress, but as he reached the last one, she pushed him away.

'No, Jonathan, don't!'

He let her go immediately, and she waited for him to get angry and say, 'For God's sake grow up, Susan. We should be in bed together, and not standing here necking like two kids,' But being Jonathan, of course he didn't.

'Not feeling in the mood, sweetheart?' he asked kindly.

'Just a bit queasy,' she lied. 'All those courses must have got mixed up on the dance floor.'

'Have you any Alka-Seltzer?'

'Yes.' She didn't, but it was easier to fib than have him fussing around like a mother hen.

'I'll call you in the morning, to see how you are,' he said at the doorway, and kissed her goodnight.

Undressing for bed, Susan knew she must stop lying to Jonathan, and break off their relationship. If she had not had to face him every day at work she would have done so on her return from America. But it was unfair to go on putting it off, and she made up her mind to tell him on Monday, the night before she left for Brocklehurst, when he had arranged to take her out for dinner again. Being away from the office for two months would ease over the difficulties, and with a bit of luck, he might have found himself another girl by the time she returned.

With her conscience clear, she slept like a log, and did not awaken until after eleven. Instead of dressing, as she usually did, and walking to the corner shop to buy the papers, she decided to take a leisurely bath and wash her hair.

An hour later, feeling thoroughly relaxed, she returned to the living room. Her hair, soft and shiny, hung down past her shoulders, and as always when she wore it this way, she derived a sensual pleasure from running her fingers between the long strands.

Tightening the belt of her dressing gown, she settled on the couch and opened the file she had brought home with her from the office. The papers could wait until later this afternoon. Barely had she started to absorb the details of yet another rather sordid divorce case, than the door bell rang.

It was probably Jonathan, she thought irritably. He only lived a few minutes away and had probably decided to call and see how she was.

But when she opened the front door, she gave a gasp of surprise, for it was not Jonathan's light grey eyes that met her own, but the sparkling, periwinkle-blue ones of Gregg Saville.

He was dressed in the inevitable jeans—Calvin Klein this time, the designer's label told her—worn with a red polo cashmere sweater that matched the quilted lining of his denim battledress jacket. His hair was ruffled, as though he had run his hands through it, and because of its unruliness the blondest strands, that normally fell forward, were now visible among the darker gold hair. Inexplicably Susan knew an urge to feel the texture, and was immediately angry at the thought.

'Good morning,' he drawled. 'Ready for me to take pictures for the *Playmate* centrefold?'

'Like hell!' she glared at him. 'What do you want?'

'Would a cup of coffee be too much?'

Ungraciously she ushered him into the lounge. The folds of her dressing gown twisted beneath her feet and she would have tripped had not two firm hands come out to steady her. Because she was not wearing slippers she was more than ever conscious of his height, and she pulled quickly from him and sat in an armchair.

'What do you really want?' she asked.

'I was passing, and thought I'd pop in and say hullo.'

'Passing by to where? You live in Eaton Place.'

'I'm coming from, as it happens,' he replied smoothly, and leaned against the mantelpiece, arms folded. 'I spent the night with some friends in Totteridge.'

'Rather a heavy night, if those dark patches under your eyes are anything to go by,' she commented, eyeing him critically.

'You don't exactly look like Miss World yourself,'

he grinned, and went on looking at her.

She knew he was hoping for some sign of discomfort, but though her cheeks burned at his scrutiny, she refused to give way to embarrassment. What did it matter if she looked a sight, with her hair clinging damply to her neck, and an old brushed wool dressing gown around her? She was not competing for his attention with anyone.

'Would you care for a drink?' she asked, deciding it would be impolite not to offer a modicum of hospitality.

He hesitated, and lowered his eyes, as if embarrassed. "I—er—I'm not alone,' he said finally. 'I've got someone downstairs in the car. In fact, that's the main reason for calling on you. I wanted you to meet her.'

'Oh.'

'She's the cutest little redhead,' he went on enthusiastically, 'and I've decided to take her to Brocklehurst with me.'

Susan wondered why this announcement did not give her more pleasure; after all, now his attention was certain to be focused elsewhere.

'Cuter than Honey?' she enquired in dulcet tones, remembering the redheaded nymphet in Los Angeles.

'Infinitely so.' He grinned impudently. 'And younger.'

'I didn't know they came much younger without breaking the law of consent!' she said sarcastically, recalling that Honey had not looked much more than eighteen or nineteen.

'My friends assured me her mother wouldn't raise any objections, so I guess she must be of age,' he said carelessly.

'Well, I suggest you don't leave her on her own a moment longer. I can wait until Tuesday for the pleasure of meeting her.'

'That's a pity.' Gregg looked crestfallen. 'Her

tongue's hanging out to meet *you*.'

Susan couldn't think why. 'When did *you* meet *her*? I only saw you a few days ago.'

'You know how it is,' he said offhandedly, 'when these things happen, they happen fast. She was staying at my friends', and it was wham, bam, love at first sight for both of us.'

'Does that account for the way you look?'

'You're damn right. The little bitch wouldn't leave me alone all night.' In spite of the rather abusive term he used to describe her, Susan could hear genuine affection in his voice. 'She woke me up three times, kissing my face and begging——'

'I don't want to hear the sordid details,' Susan cut in hastily, sickened that he seemed so willing to discuss them with her. Was nothing about his love-life sacred?

'Well, how about it?' he cajoled winsomely. 'May I bring her up and introduce her?'

'I really can't see the purpose,' she protested.

'You will,' he stated matter-of-factly. 'Now why don't you dry your hair and get dressed, then we can all go for a walk on the Heath before lunch. It's a glorious day.'

'Two's company,' she stated firmly. 'I wouldn't dream of intruding.'

'You won't be,' he assured her. 'Anyway, I made it clear to her that I don't believe in a one-for-one relationship, so if she's upset——'

'You really are a cold-blooded bastard, aren't you?' Susan rounded on him furiously, then stood up, feeling at a disadvantage having to tilt her head back to look at him. Yet even when she was on her feet he still towered over her. 'You don't know the meaning of the word love. She's a new toy, nothing more.'

'Perhaps.' His tone was offhand. 'But I'll sure enjoy playing with her at Brocklehurst!'

'You're disgusting!'

'And you're beautiful. There are bright red patches on your cheeks. It makes you look even more like a little girl than that ridiculously old-fashioned dressing-gown.'

He let his gaze wander slowly over the length of her, and suddenly conscious that she was naked beneath it, Susan drew the belt tighter around the waist.

As he saw the movement, his smile widened, and he touched the fleecy material. 'It looks like something my grandmother used to wear, though I have to admit it does rather more for you!'

'Thanks!' she retorted, and then suddenly found she was smiling too. 'As it happens, it was *my* grandmother's. I borrowed it so many times when I went to stay with her, she decided to give it to me and buy herself another one.'

'It's certainly a lot more practical than the flimsy things women generally prance around in.'

Your women anyway, she thought, and immediately visualised the redhead in his car waltzing in front of him in silk and lace. Hastily she blanked out the image, and moved a few paces towards her bedroom door.

'I'll get dressed,' she said.

'Good. And I'll go and fetch her ladyship. I'll leave the door open—it will save you the trouble of answering it.'

Within five minutes Susan had changed into straight-legged trousers in fine mossy brown suede and a long-sleeved wool shirt and jacket in mid-brown. It was one of her favourite outfits, and one of the most expensive too.

She spent another few minutes drying her hair and then caught it back in a ponytail. Without any softness to frame her face, her features were clearly seen; the wide, well-shaped mouth, the line of her firmly rounded chin, and the large blue-green eyes, framed by thick, dark blonde lashes.

Because she did not care what she looked like, she wore no make-up—though if this were true, she argued with her usual honesty, as she stared at her reflection, why had she chosen one of her smartest outfits instead of the jeans and sloppy sweater she usually sported on Sundays? It was as inexplicable as the pink glow that had crept into her skin, or the high colour of her cheeks that emphasised the delicate hollows beneath them.

Quietly she re-entered the living room, steeling herself to be pleasant. After all, Gregg Saville's new girl-friend could hardly be blamed for his unheralded intrusion on her free Sunday.

Surprisingly, there was no sign of anyone other than the man himself.

'I deduce your girl-friend wasn't as anxious to meet me as you supposed?' Susan said sarcastically as she surveyed the empty room.

'Wrong again, Watson,' he grinned. 'She just got tired of waiting, and fell asleep. I put her over there by the couch.'

Perplexed, Susan shook her head. 'What on earth——'

'Go over and take a look,' he instructed, indicating a large cardboard box on the floor.

Stunned, Susan looked and then rounded on him. 'That's the most miserable, dirty, rotten, trick anyone's played on me!'

But her anger was only feigned, and impossible to sustain when faced by the most adorable red-setter puppy she had ever seen, who lay curled up in a ball on an old pink satin-edged baby blanket.

'And because you're so eager to think the worst of me, you fell for it, hook, line and sinker.' Gregg smiled back at her. Then his smile widened and he started to laugh; deep belly laughs that were contagious, so that Susan was engulfed too.

After a couple of minutes, the noise awakened the puppy, who stretched, yawned, wagged her tail, clambered out of the box, and immediately squatted down and made a tiny puddle on the carpet.

'Oops!' Gregg scolded, scooping her up in his hands, while Susan dashed into the kitchen for a J-cloth. 'How can you expect to impress Susan with your charms if you disgrace yourself like that?'

For answer, she licked his hand as he placed her back in the box, and immediately scrambled out again.

'Her paws are too big, and so are her ears, and her tail reminds me of a rat,' Susan commented, watching as the puppy played tug-of-war with the fringe of a rug. 'But it's love at first sight for me too!'

'What shall we call her?'

'Don't rush me. That needs careful thought.'

'Well, I have all day. How about you?'

She hesitated. 'I have to go over a file I brought home with me.'

'I'll get you back in time to do it, I promise.'

'Okay,' she acquiesced. 'But how can we walk the puppy on the Heath without a lead and collar—or have you got them?'

'Not yet, so we'll have to carry her.'

'Has she had all her injections—just in case we do put her down for a few minutes?'

'Yes—and she's also been wormed.'

'I assume her mother was owned by your friends?' Susan asked, as they went down the stairs, the puppy nestling against Gregg's shoulder like a baby about to be burped, while she carried its box.

He nodded. 'She was mated with the triple champion of England, so on her father's side her pedigree is almost as good as mine!'

The puppy dozed off on Susan's knee until they

reached Kenwood—where he was forced to park on
the main road, as the car park was full because of the
sunshine and the blue skies—and they then took turns
carrying her, each reluctant to give her up to the other.

'I can see why divorced couples often fight for
custody of the dog,' Gregg laughed, as they reached
the lake.

They circled round it into the woods, where the
autumn leaves carpeting the pathways almost exactly
matched the setter's silky fur, and then made their way
back via the terrace of Kenwood House itself, so they
could admire the view.

'You seem to know your way around as well as I
do,' Susan commented.

'I've been coming to London for more years than I
care to remember,' he replied, 'and I have friends who
live over the way in The Bishop's Avenue.'

'You never stay with friends, though?'

'Not for want of asking, I assure you. But I prefer to
be independent.' He placed the puppy on the grass,
but did not release her. 'Do you think she'd run away
if I let go of her? I'd like her to spend another penny
before we go back to the car.'

'There's only one way to find out,' Susan smiled.

The puppy seemed a little frightened, but after a
couple of minutes she obliged, and they both praised
her lavishly.

'The housekeeper at my apartment will be happy to
see the back of me on Tuesday,' Gregg commented, as
they approached the car. 'Silk Persian rugs and
Aubusson carpets weren't meant for the likes of this
young lady.'

'Keep her locked up in the kitchen,' Susan
suggested. 'Or perhaps the super-rich like yourself
have Aubussen in the kitchen too!'

He smiled. 'That's good advice. I'm afraid I have to
admit to never having trained a puppy myself. I've

always had staff to do it for me.'

'Well, once you get her down to Brocklehurst, you won't have to worry. They've always had dogs there, and the maids are used to coping.'

He set the Rolls in motion, and with a careful eye on the traffic, did a U-turn, so that they were facing the way they had come.

'Hampstead isn't exactly the Mecca of good food,' he remarked, 'so I thought we'd go into town to eat. How does the Connaught sound to you?'

'Fine. I'm hungry enough to eat a horse!'

'The head waiter knows me well, and if that's what you want, I'm sure he'll be happy to oblige!'

Leaving the puppy in its box, he parked near the entrance of the red brick hotel, where once again the doorman greeted him like a long-lost friend and teased him about his new status, as did the staff in the cosy panelled bar.

It was three o'clock before they returned to the car, where the puppy was still fast asleep.

'They're like babies at this age,' Susan commented. 'They sleep for about twenty hours a day.'

'Thank goodness. I was worried what tricks she might have got up to. This car isn't mine, remember?'

Susan smiled as she looked at the puppy, who was now trying to climb out of her box and on to the back seat.

'I think we'd better get her to perform her favourite trick before we go any further,' she suggested. 'She's been in here for two hours.'

To their relief the puppy instantly obliged in the curb of the road.

'She's a regular little lady,' Gregg drawled. 'Well behaved and adorable.'

'That's it!' Susan exclaimed. 'You've found the name. Why not call her Lady?'

'Lady?' he echoed. 'That's not bad. Yes, not bad at

all. That's what she'll be, then—Lady!'

With the newly christened puppy sitting in Susan's lap, they returned to her flat, where, in a far from ladylike manner, the little dog devoured a large bowl of Weetabix. Then, stomach bulging, she explored the flat thoroughly before clambering back into her box and settling down to sleep.

'Well, now the baby's resting, I think we deserve a cup of coffee,' said Susan, and disappeared into the kitchen to put on the percolator.

'This is good,' said Gregg a few minutes later as he sampled it. 'Almost American.'

'You all háve a thing about your coffee!' she teased.

'Understandably. No one outside the States know how to make it. It always tastes different in Europe.'

'The only difference is in the water. The chlorine and lime content varies from country to country.'

'You sound as if you've made a study of it,' he commented.

'There was an article about it in the papers a couple of days ago,' Susan confessed.

'You have a nice flat,' Gregg commented, as she offered him a chocolate peppermint cream. 'I like the way you've done it.'

'Habitat, and junk shop Victoriana, renovated by my father,' she told him. 'It's his hobby.'

She poured herself coffee too, and curled up in the couch opposite, aware of his appraisal.

'For a girl on a limited budget you also dress well,' he told her.

'Thank you,' she said, pleased at the compliments, though wondering at the same time if they were leading up to something more. 'They're also bargain basement. I rarely buy anything other than in a sale.'

'There's nothing wrong with buying wisely, as long as you buy well. That outfit of yours may have been a bargain, but I bet it didn't come from C & A!'

'Browns, actually,' she smiled.

He set his coffee cup down, and as he returned to his former position in the seat of the small tub chair, she thought what a ridiculous picture his powerful-looking body made, framed against the dainty flowers of the Laura Ashley print.

'It's a pity you have to work tonight,' he went on. 'We could have gone to see a movie and then had dinner.'

'That would have been nice,' she agreed, and meant it. 'But I really do have to get through that file.'

'How about tomorrow, then?'

'I'm sorry, I have a date.'

'Girl friend or boy-friend?' he questioned.

'Boy-friend.'

'Competition, or is it platonic?'

This was beginning to sound like an inquisition. 'I wasn't aware you were a competitor, Mr Saville,' she answered.

'Well, my interest in you sure as hell isn't platonic!' he smiled, 'and I thought we'd agreed you were going to call me Gregg.'

'I'm sorry, but I find it difficult to think of you as Gregg.'

In a swift movement he stood up and crossed to sit beside her, then before she had a chance to resist him, he gathered her into his arms.

'Perhaps this will help,' he said, as his mouth came full down on hers.

It was warm and gentle, as were his hands that moved down her back to her waist, drawing her close against him. Susan felt the heat radiating from his body and breathed in the spicy scent of after-shave lotion, and the more intimate smell of the man himself. She struggled to free herself, but his grip tightened, his fingers digging into her flesh. This was the first close physical contact they had had, and as she fought to be free of him she was conscious of his strength. It was like fighting a wall of steel. He pushed her back against the softness of the cushions, so that she was half-lying and pinned her there with his body. Her brain was a jumble of chaotic thought, as were her emotions, though soon one began to take precedence over the other as his kisses grew deeper and more demanding, arousing her to a response she did not want to give, yet was unable to withhold. His hands ran up beneath her, and gently played along her spine, and each single vertebra came alive under his touch, with sensations she would never have believed existed.

'Gregg,' she mumbled, but his lips were fastened on hers and she could not speak properly.

'Be quiet,' he muttered, lifting his mouth fractionally. 'Don't you know there's a time for silence?'

Once more he was kissing her, one hand gripping her close the other reaching beneath her to free her hair. His fingers untied the ribbon, and the blonde tresses spread around her shoulders. He murmured something incomprehensible and placed his hand on the nape of her neck, rubbing the soft skin, and arousing her to even greater heights of desire, so that she was unaware of everything except his mouth and hands; now undoing the buttons of her blouse, now releasing her breasts; sucking, kissing, licking, rubbing, holding, until she knew that only the ultimate act of sex would bring the release she craved.

'Susan,' he said thickly, and half raised himself away from her. 'My beautiful Susan.'

His face was above her, so near that she saw the skin had a discernible texture. There was a flush on the high cheekbones and the glitter of passion in the narrowed eyes. Those same eyes which had gazed with passion at countless other women, all of whom had meant as little to him as she would herself, when passion was spent. Brought to her senses by her thoughts, she pushed him roughly away, and rolled from beneath him. At once she distanced herself from him, and clutching her blouse around her to cover her nakedness, she came to rest by the fireplace.

'Why did you do that?' Gregg asked huskily.

'Because I didn't want to go on with something I had no intention of finishing.' Her voice was shaky, and she swallowed hard.

He stood up, and came to stand near her. His heightened colour made his skin look more bronzed, and as she watched him he ran a hand over his head, ruffling the blond-flecked hair in the front.

'Why not? You were enjoying it as much as I was.'

'I don't deny it. But I'm not interested in being just another statistic in your life.'

'Is that how you think I'd regard you?' His lids which had been lowered lifted, showing glittering blue eyes that had deepened to cobalt with passion.

'Why should you treat me differently from any other woman?'

He moved nearer, and lightly traced the bones of her face with his index finger; the short, straight nose, the high cheekbones, the rounded jawline. It was a tender gesture, and totally unexpected, but Susan refused to see it as anything but a ploy to make her believe she meant something more to him than a pleasant interlude.

'I have no intention of going to bed with you even if you tell me you love me,' she said coolly. 'I've been around enough to know a line when I hear one.'

'Why are you so certain that's all I have in mind?'

'Don't tell me you're going to deny it's been your intention from the first day we met?'

He dropped his hand and stepped back. 'I don't deny it. You're very fanciable.'

'And as I've told you many times before, you aren't.'

'In which case you deserve an Academy Award for the performance you put on a few moments ago.'

Susan went scarlet, but bravely met his mocking gaze. 'You're a professional, Gregg. If you put your mind to it, you could melt an iceberg.'

'What are you made of—stone?' he questioned irritably.

'Where you're concerned—yes. I thought I'd made myself perfectly clear on that point. But just in case I haven't, I'll do so now.' Her voice firmed. 'I'm not interested in one-night stands, or even two-month stands for that matter, if that's what you had in mind. You can relieve your boredom with Davina—or are you already tired of her?'

His eyes flickered, but he did not answer. Instead he turned away and moved over to the dining-table, where he had draped his jacket over one of the chairs.

'I'd like to get down to Brocklehurst in time for lunch on Tuesday,' he said casually as he eased himself into it. 'I believe it's about a two-hour run, so perhaps you could call for me at ten.'

Susan admired his cool. Obviously it took more than a verbal slap in the face to disarm a man of his experience.

'That suits me fine,' she answered with equal panache.

He picked up the box containing Lady, and walked with her to the flat door, and Susan—after hastily doing up the buttons of her blouse—followed.

'Do you mind if I ask you a question?' said Gregg, as she opened it.

'I don't promise to answer it.'

'Did you just say what you did because you don't like me, or because you're frightened you like me too much?'

Was there no end to the conceit of this man? She searched for an answer that would put him in his place. 'What do you think?' she said finally, the question rhetorical, her voice as sweet as honey. 'I'm absolutely petrified of falling in love with you!'

'That's exactly what I thought.'

His insolent smile made her wish face-slapping had not gone out with long skirts. 'You are without doubt the most infuriating man I've ever met!' she snapped.

Leaning forward, he kissed her swiftly on the lips. 'I know. But I simply adore you!'

In spite of the box, he took the stairs two at the time, and she leaned over the banisters and watched him until he disappeared from view.

The insistent ringing of the telephone drew her back to the living-room, and she was not surprised, when she answered it, to hear Jonathan's irritated voice on the other end.

'Where on earth have you been?' he demanded. 'I called round at twelve to see how you were, and to ask you out for lunch.'

A lie formed and then dissolved. 'Someone else asked me first,' she said. 'Gregg—Mr Saville popped in to show me a red-setter puppy he'd bought, and one thing led to another.'

'Did it really?' he said nastily.

'Look, Jonathan, I don't have a contract with you that says I can't go out with anyone else. So stop acting as if you've been cuckolded!'

'I can't help it, Susan,' he sounded contrite. 'You know how I feel about you, and it drives me crazy to think of you with another man—particularly *that* one.'

'Look,' she said wearily, 'I don't want to discuss it now. I have the Granger file to go through, and I really do want to get a start.'

'Okay,' he agreed. 'But I'd like to discuss it with you over dinner tomorrow. I think it's about time we got out future settled.'

Poor Jonathan! In spite of the lacklustre way she

had been acting towards him, he probably still believed she would say yes to him in the end. It was a shame that she couldn't. He was such a nice man. Nice. Susan turned the word over in her mind. What a mundane description it was, and how terribly boring. It was a word one could never apply to Gregg Saville. Irritating, conceited, opinionated, irrepressible, faithless, these were the right adjectives. But goodness, however unflattering, they made him one hell of an interesting guy to be with!

Dangerous too, she thought more soberly, as staring at her reflection in the bedroom mirror, she saw that her mouth was still so red from his kisses that she looked as if she was wearing lipstick. His lovemaking had told her how easy it would be to have an affair with him, but an affair that could lead to nowhere, and end with nothing but heartache, for once committed, there was always the possibility that she might fall in love with him. Fall in love with a man she despised? It was not impossible. Whatever his faults, there were also his virtues, and when he was in the mood to display them, he could make her forget everything else.

CHAPTER EIGHT

By the time Tuesday morning arrived, in spite of her misgivings about spending the next two months in Gregg's company, Susan was relieved to leave London and the office behind her. Her dinner with Jonathan had been a painful one; painful because she could see how much he loved her and wanted to marry her, and because when he had finally realised it was all over between them, he had been close to tears.

She made Eaton Place by five to ten, and managed to find a meter right outside Gregg's apartment block—an imposing one, but of pre-war vintage.

She had been hoping to find him waiting for her in the entrance hall, but the only man in sight was the porter.

'I've come to collect Mr Saville,' she said. 'Could you phone and tell him I'm here?'

'Whom should I tell *His Grace* is calling?' the man asked snootily.

'Miss Goody-Goody,' Susan told him with a perfectly straight face.

Without so much as an eyebrow raised in surprise, the man did as she requested. Hyphenated names were no doubt two a penny in this area, she mused, and his training, like that of a good butler, had taught him not to show surprise at anything he saw or heard.

Gregg appeared within a few minutes with Lady in his arms, accompanied by an elderly manservant carrying a large black leather Hermes suitcase in each hand.

'These will never fit in my boot,' she greeted Gregg, 'so we'll have to put them on the back seat.'

'It's great to see you too!' he grinned. Obviously their little contretemps on Sunday had had no dampening effect on his spirits, and he bore no animosity. Or perhaps, more worryingly, he had just not taken her seriously?

'Grieves, this is Miss Andrews,' he introduced them.

The elderly man smiled warmly. 'Aren't you the young lady we have to thank for finding Mr Saville?'

'You see,' said Gregg, as the man disappeared inside again. 'Not everyone dislikes me, and as you know servants are notoriously good judges of character.'

'That's about as true as dogs and children knowing who likes them. They always make a beeline for those who don't!'

'In the mood you're in, I think it might be better if *I* drove,' he chuckled.

'It's *my* car, and *I'll* drive it.'

'How nice to be back to our old relationship.' Eyes as blue as the Mediterranean glinted at her. 'I find sparring with you almost as stimulating as making love!'

'In that case, I shall be as docile as a lamb, and agree with everything you say!'

'I'll believe that when I hear it!'

His size looked even more overwhelming in the confines of her baby Renault, and even with the passenger seat pushed back as far as it would go, he was forced to sit with his long legs slightly bunched.

But Lady had no difficulty finding a comfortable position, and after a few minutes sniffing the dashboard and window, she fell off to sleep.

'How was she?' Susan asked.

'Let's put it like this. If she's not house-trained before her next visit, I think I'll have to book a room for the two of us at the Berkeley!'

Susan couldn't help smiling. 'It will be easier to

confine her to the kitchen quarters at Brocklehurst, and she'll have all the grounds to exercise in as well. I'm sure everyone will love her.'

'I hope they feel as much good-will towards me,' he commented.

'A bit apprehensive, are you?'

'Believe it or not, I'm not devoid of all emotions,' he said dryly.

She reddened. 'I wasn't aware I'd suggested you were.'

'I thought you were going to agree with everything I said?' he smiled.

'I've decided it would be impossible—and rather boring.'

'Even docile, you wouldn't bore me, Susan,' he said softly.

'Don't you ever take no for an answer?' she asked, exasperated.

'What's that supposed to mean?'

'Stop flirting with me.'

'I wasn't flirting with you, just telling you the truth. The trouble is you have such a one-sided view of me, you can't—or you don't want to—see the difference.'

She decided it would be better not to answer, as the conversation might start to get out of hand again, and the next half hour or so passed in silence. By that time they had left London behind them, and the motorway stretched ahead.

It was a fine day, rather than a sunny one, and still warm for the time of year, and Susan wore an ochre and khaki checked knibed jacket, pale olive crêpe-de-chine shirt with a green and rush matchstick print, and a matching plaid knife-pleated skirt. Whatever Davina greeted them in, she would not feel like the poor relation.

Covertly she eyed the man at her side. She had not

studied him profile on before, and she saw that his hair grew longer on the nape of his neck, the ends a paler bronze, like the strands that fell across his forehead. He had beautifully shaped ears, the tips very slightly pointed. Was that a sign of intuition, or did it signify humour? Certainly he had shown plenty of both where she was concerned.

'I saw that article about you in the *Sunday Times* magazine,' she said conversationally. 'Someone brought it into the office yesterday to show me. Why didn't you tell me they'd been over to Los Angeles to interview you?'

'I'm so used to being interviewed, I didn't think to mention it.'

'But you did see it?'

'Yes. I thought it was rather good—and not in the least snide.' Gregg tickled the puppy's ears gently with his forefinger, and she wriggled contentedly. 'They're doing a follow-up in a couple of months, down at Brocklehurst,' he went on. 'They want to see how I've adapted myself to my new role.'

'Don't you find it rather a bore—being interviewed, I mean?'

'Not when the questions are intelligent.'

'What about being recognised?'

'Until all this recent publicity about me, I rarely was over here. But back home, of course, I have something like star status.' He half smiled. 'I have to admit to rather enjoying it, and I think that most people in the same position would say the same thing. It gets you the best tables in restaurants, V.I.P. treatment at airports and hotels, and one never has any trouble finding staff. But best of all, it acts as a sort of aphrodisiac on women.'

Sex again! Susan fumed, but hid it.

'With your looks, I would have thought your fame entirely immaterial to your success rate!'

'My, my,' he mocked. 'That's almost sounds like a compliment!'

'I can't deny the truth, Gregg. You're a very good-looking man.'

'But not the kind of looks *you* go for?'

Was he mocking her again? 'Looks aren't important to me' she said. 'It's the qualities of a man that count.'

'Don't I have *any* you admire?'

'No one can be all bad!'

He laughed. 'Will you tell me what my virtues are—other than the fact that I kiss with expertise?'

'I don't like to have to think too hard about anything when I'm driving, but I promise when I have the time I'll write them down on a postage stamp and let you have them!'

He laughed again. 'Always ready with the right reply, aren't you?' He shifted around in the seat, and made an attempt to stretch his legs out in front of him.

'Is this advance discourager your own, or did you borrow it for self-preservation?' he went on.

She looked at him in puzzlement. 'It's my own,' she said, 'but what is an advance discourager?'

'The sort of car that stops you starting something it's a physical impossibility to finish unless you're a midget!'

She smiled. 'It's a comforting thought to know I'm safe. Instead of locking my door at night, as protection from you, I'll sleep in here!'

'I wouldn't dream of entering a young lady's bedroom uninvited,' he said in mock horror. 'And in any case, I have Davina to relieve my boredom.'

She deserved that, she admitted to herself. Her remark about Davina had been bitchy, and she had regretted it as soon as she had made it.

The next hour went by mostly in silence, with Gregg passing the odd comment about the scenery. She was not sorry. Their conversations always seemed to take a personal turn, no matter what subject they started out discussing, and she was too aware of the danger inherent in furthering their intimacy to feel relaxed.

'We turn off in about five minutes,' Susan told him, as they crossed the spaghetti junction at Birmingham, 'and then it's about another twenty minutes, depending on the traffic. The roads aren't very good, and in this weather it will be impossible to overtake if we get stuck behind a lorry.'

It had started to cloud over after Coventry, and it was now raining fairly hard. The temperature had dropped suddenly too, and she had turned on the heater.

It was fortunate she knew the road well, for after they left the motorway, a low mist also fell, and it would have been easy to miss the sign for the A436 that led to Henley-in-Arden, and past it to Brocklehurst.

'You're seeing everything at its worst,' Susan commented, as they passed through a particularly pretty village.

'It doesn't really matter. I'm here for a while, and I can always drive back to see what I've missed.'

'But first impressions are so important.'

'That depends. I'm sure you don't dislike me anywhere near as much now as you did the first time we met.'

'Do you always have to put everything in personal terms?' she asked crossly.

'Where you're concerned—yes.'

'I thought I'd made my position where *you're* concerned perfectly clear on Sunday?'

'When a girl responds to me the way you did, I don't give up easily.'

'I could always walk out on you?' she threatened.

'But you won't, will you?' he stated matter-of-factly.

No, damn it, I can't. Mr Maddox would be furious,

apart from my more personal considerations.'

'Of course,' he agreed silkily. 'But if I hadn't thought you would be of real help to me, I wouldn't have insisted you came down here.'

'I'd like to believe that,' Susan said sourly.

'I won't deny the idea of killing two birds with one stone didn't appeal to me,' he went on, as if she had not spoken. 'But seducing you was not uppermost in my mind. If I simply wanted sex, I have plenty of girls I could call on.'

Was he trying to suggest that his interest in her was not purely a physical one? It sounded like it. But she was too suspicious of him to accept what he said at face value. Perhaps realising now she meant what she said about forming casual relationships, he had decided a change of tactics was called for. He might even pretend he had fallen in love with her.

'Why don't I tell you something of the history of the house,' she said, abruptly changing the subject. 'We'll be at the village soon.'

'Go ahead,' he said agreeably, and looked amused. 'I can take a hint!'

'The title was bestowed by Henry the Eighth in 1530,' she began, 'and with it came vast tracts of land, and the wherewithal to build the house. It was started in 1531, but unfortunately the first Duke didn't live long enough to see its completion, nor enjoy opening its doors to Queen Elizabeth the First.'

'You sound as if you're reciting that off by heart,' he remarked, as she paused to make a right turn.

'I am,' she confessed. 'For three years I worked as a guide during my summer holidays from school.' It was during this time that Charles had begun to take more than passing interest in her, but she had no intention of telling this to Gregg. She continued with her potted history lesson. 'Brocklehurst continued to play host to royalty until it was destroyed by fire in 1621, and it was the fourth Duke who took upon himself the task of recreating not only a great house, but a great heritage. He commissioned Inigo Jones to rebuild it. He also started the collection of art and furniture that you see there today.'

'What about the village? Does that date as far back?'

'Seventeenth and eighteenth century mostly,' she replied, 'but as the rain appears to be stopping, you'll be able to see for yourself. We're here.'

One of the loveliest villages in the country, Brocklehurst was set on the slope of a hill, with a round pond at the bottom, complete with a thatched shelter for ducks, geese and swans. Thatched cottages, as well as attractive weatherboarded and tile-hung houses on narrow pavements, led to a small, wide High Street, fringed by trees and grass, immaculately kept by the residents. There was one pub, the Duke's Head, which was genuine Elizabethan, but the shops, though timbered in the same style, were mainly Georgian.

'Even on a day as damp and wet as this, it looks idyllic,' Gregg commented, as they reached the top of the hill, and he turned round to admire the view from the back window. 'And just look at that church!' he exclaimed as they passed the creeper-covered building, angled so that it was in full view of anyone entering the village.

'Just outside the walls are stocks and whipping posts,' Susan told him. 'Sometimes I think it wouldn't be a bad idea if the stocks were still in use. It might do a few of the hooligans good to be humiliated as they were in the old days.'

'It would be a damn sight more sensible than shutting them away with hardened criminals who encourage them to continue a life of crime, and teach them all the tricks of the trade.'

'We're fortunate here,' Susan told him. 'We don't even have a village policeman. It's such a close-knit community that no one would dream of stealing anything. It would be like robbing a member of one's own family.'

'What about in the summer, with the tourists? Don't you ever have any trouble there?'

'For the peak two months of July and August, we share a policeman with the next village. It's only ten minutes away. But the security people up at the house manage to deal with most problems. Don't think we don't have any crime round here, though,' she added. 'There are some very expensive homes, and they're constantly being burgled. But that's handled by the regional crime squad.'

They had now reached the end of the narrow leafy lane that lead to the house, and she drove through the huge wrought iron gates that proclaimed the main entrance.

'Well, this is it,' she announced proudly. 'And I hope you learn to love it as much as all your ancestors.'

If first impressions were anything to go by, the signs were hopeful, for if Gregg has been enamoured by the village, he was rendered almost speechless by the beauty of Brocklehurst itself.

Set amidst rolling parkland, that stretched as far as the eye could see, it stood three storeys high, and was built of mellowed grey stone. Its long white-painted windows, arched entrance and squarely angled bays gave it a Gothic appearance, that was further emphasised by the crenellated surround of the flat roof. The front steps leading to the wide balustraded and paved terrace that went all around the house were guarded by two huge stone lions, as were those leading to French windows at the sides and rear, where there was a swimming pool, tennis courts, and magnificent formal gardens leading down to a lake.

Davina, looking every inch a duchess in full-skirted blue chiffon—more suited to a summer evening's party than lunch on a damp winter's day, Susan thought cattily—flowed down the stone steps to greet Gregg.

'Dear Gregg,' she said warmly, kissing him chastely on the cheek. 'Welcome to your new home.'

'It's nice to be here,' Susan heard him reply, as she gave chase to Lady, whom he had deposited on the gravel, but who had decided the lawns looked far more interesting.

'Is that yours?' Davina asked, as she returned, slightly breathless.

'No, she's mine,' Gregg intervened. 'Her name's Lady, and she's nine weeks old.'

'She's an adorable little thing.' Davina leaned across to pet the puppy's head.

'But not yet house-trained, I'm afraid,' Gregg informed her. 'It might be best if one of the staff took her over until she is.'

It was no sooner said than done, and the puppy was handed over to one of the young maids, who was lined up in the hall with the rest of the staff, to meet the new Duke.

Gregg spoke to them all, asking their names and what their particular job was, and watching him, appearing completely at ease, Susan could not but help admire him. He exhibited the same cool charm and lack of pretension he had shown to the staff at the Berkeley and Connaught, and it was obvious they were warming to him in the same way.

But today it was not only his manners she admired, but the way he was dressed. She had not commented on it, but she had been pleased to see he was not wearing his inevitable jeans. Instead, he had obviously paid a visit to an excellent tailoring establishment.

Whether he had followed their advice or it was his own choice, he looked every inch an English aristocrat, in cinnamon corduroy tapered trousers, cream shirt worn with a plain brown woollen tie, and a vented single-breasted jacket in a tweed mixture of all three shades with suede-patched elbows. If she could pick any fault, it was that he looked almost too smart, his clothes too new. But short of buying them in a second-hand shop, there was no way round that particular problem!

'I've put you in the East Wing,' Davina told Susan as the staff disbanded, leaving the butler and a young man to escort them to their rooms and carry up their luggage.

There was a discreet cough from Danvers.

'The central heating hasn't been working too well in the East Wing, Your Grace,' he said, addressing Davina, 'so I took the liberty of preparing a room for Miss Susan in the West Wing.'

Susan knew the East Wing was the servants' quarters, and she wondered if Danvers was telling the truth. But looking at his poker face, there was no way of telling.

'Very sensible of you,' Davina commended, but Susan noticed a slight tightening of the rosebud lips, denoting that she was far from pleased.

The butler turned to Gregg. 'If you'll follow me, Your Grace, I'll show you to your room. I've prepared the master bedroom for you, naturally.'

'Fine,' said Gregg. 'But there is one thing I'd like to make clear, Danvers. I prefer to be addressed as Mr Saville, and I'd be obliged if you'd inform the rest of the staff of my wishes.'

If the butler was surprised, he was far too well trained to show it. 'As you wish, sir.'

'Harry will unpack for you, Gregg,' said Davina, referring to the young man standing patiently by the luggage at the foot of the staircase. 'So why not just go up and inspect your room and make sure everything's to your liking. Then come to the library for a pre-lunch drink.' She looked towards Susan. 'I'm sure Mr Saville won't mind if you take the rest of the day off to see your parents, dear. I intend to take him round the house this afternoon, so that at least he'll have some idea of his bearings, and I've asked some friends over for dinner to meet him this evening.'

'If that's all right with Gregg. . . .' Susan looked at him questioningly.

'Of course. I was going to suggest it myself.'

They followed the butler and his young assistant up the magnificent cantilevered staircase, and down the Long Gallery, where family portraits and other works of art by many famous painters lined the walls on either side. Gainsborough, Romney, Holbein, Van Dyck, they were all here in a private collection that many an art gallery might envy.

'I really *do* resemble them,' Gregg commented. 'And we seem to have more than just our looks in common, if their wives are an indication of their taste, and not just arranged marriages. Even by today's standards, one could call them beautiful.'

'But none more beautiful than Davina,' Susan said, as he paused to admire her picture, painted by Annigoni.

'You took the words right out of my mouth.'

Her bedroom was two doors away from his, and contained a magnificent fourposter bed, richly embellished with appliqué. The walls were covered in the same silk, the furniture gilded, and the chairs and footstools in needlework that blended perfectly with the soft pastel shades of the floral carpet. Although opulent, it had an air of faded grandeur, as did the small en-suite bathroom. But hot water gushed from the taps, and there were plenty of large, fluffy towels, which was all that really mattered.

Susan was in the midst of unpacking when there was a knock at the door, and almost before she had time to say 'come in', Gregg did so.

'How's the room?' he asked. 'Better than the servants' quarters?'

'How did you know they were in the East Wing?' she asked in surprise.

'An educated guess,' he smiled. 'Or to put it another way I know women.'

'What's that supposed to mean?'

'You're a very pretty girl,' he said, matter-of-factly, 'and Davina has her eye on me for hubby number two.'

'Are you interested?' Susan asked more casually than she felt.

He shrugged. 'You know my feelings about marriage. But I have to admit that if I do decide to keep the estate and house, I'll need a wife.' He seated himself on the edge of the bed. 'Davina would be a perfect choice, don't you agree?'

Susan lifted a dress out of her case, and slipped it on a padded satin hanger. 'I only give advice on divorce, not marriage,' she said flatly, and walked over to the wardrobe with it.

'One day I'll ask you the right question, and you'll give me a straight answer!' he said.

She returned to her case, and this time extracted a skirt and matching blouse. 'I wouldn't keep the Duchess waiting. She expected you to join her straight away.'

'I thought we'd go together. I'm afraid I forgot to ask Danvers where the library was.'

'I'll leave this till later, then,' she said, and slipped on her jacket.

'You are joining us for lunch, aren't you?' Gregg asked, as they walked back down the Long Gallery.

'I thought——'

'Well, you thought wrong—at least as far as I'm concerned,' he qualified.

One look at Davina's face told Susan she had not expected her to eat with them. The small mouth tightened, and for an instant the soft brown eyes went hard, but she recovered her equilibrium and gave her a bright smile, before ringing for Danvers to instruct him to lay another place in the dining-room.

But she did not include Susan in the conversation, if she could avoid it, and talked to Gregg as though they were alone.

'You must tell me all your likes and dislikes regarding food, so that I can ensure Cook makes your favourite dishes.'

'I'm fairly easy,' Gregg answered, 'but I have been rather spoiled by the standard of my own chef.'

'Well, this is your home, Gregg, and if you're not satisfied with Mrs Holden's efforts, it's up to you to tell her,' Davina lectured.

'Don't worry, I shall. And that goes for everything else too,' he said. 'I'll be making quite a few changes.'

'Really, darling?' Davina leaned towards Gregg, as if intent on excluding Susan completely. 'Do tell me what you have in mind?'

'I don't intend to renew the lease on the fairground, for one thing.'

'It's extremely profitable—not just the rent,' Davina pointed out. 'We get a percentage of the takings.'

'I'm well aware of that.' There was a slight edge to his voice. 'But I think we could have something equally profitable, and rather more tasteful.'

'Taste doesn't appeal to the masses.'

'That doesn't happen to be my opinion.' His voice brooked no argument. 'What do you think, Susan?'

'What have you in mind to take its place?'

'Weekends at Brocklehurst, with me as resident host.'

'You mean you've made up your mind to live here?' Susan asked in surprise.

'Only for the summer months—but that's when we can charge the highest rates.' He paused to sip his whisky. 'I reckon we could accommodate about twelve couples—it would be rather like a house-party, and that's what I'd call it—and charge a thousand pounds a couple. They'd pay that for a suite at one of the best hotels, and we'll provide everything they do and more.'

Susan calculated quickly in her head. 'That's nearly one hundred and fifty thousand pounds, if you could occupy all the rooms.'

'I've no doubt of it,' Gregg said smoothly. 'In fact, I guarantee there'll be a waiting list.'

'Won't you find it rather boring?' queried Davina. 'I mean, it might be fun for the first few weekends, but the sort of people you're bound to attract will be . . .' she hesitated, as if seeking the right words, 'unsophisticated hicks is the kindest way of putting it,' she said finally.

'Perhaps,' he agreed. 'But that doesn't necessarily make them uninteresting. And in any case, the idea is to make as much money as possible, in as short a time as possible.'

'It would cost very little to set up,' Susan commented. 'I mean, the rooms are all here, ready furnished, and——'

'Not so fast!' Gregg cut in with a smile. 'Most of the guests will be Americans who have a good deal of money, and they'll have travelled. They'll expect all the comforts of a first-class hotel.'

'I don't agree,' said Susan. 'Part of the charm of staying here will be because it's antiquated. As long as all the plumbing works, they'll love the genuine art-deco bathrooms and peeling paintwork. If you want to turn it into comfort Hilton-style, they might as well stay at one.'

Gregg looked thoughtful for a moment or two. 'You know, I think you're right. All we'll need is a few extra staff.'

'Is that why Carter was coming over here?' Susan asked.

Gregg nodded. 'And a few other modernisation schemes connected with it. But I think you've just done him out of a job.'

'Who is Carter?' Davina asked, and when Gregg told her, she nodded. 'I've heard of him.'

'I hope you won't be disappointed at not seeing him?' Gregg addressed Susan.

'If you're worried I'll be bored in the evenings, you have no need,' she replied. 'I have lots of friends round here, and I'll have plenty to do.'

She could see he was annoyed at her prevarication, because his lips tightened. But he made no comment.

'Why don't we go in for lunch, Gregg?' Davina suggested brightly. 'We can discuss your ideas at greater length this afternoon, when I take you over the house. I'm sure I'll be able to give you lots of useful advice.'

'I'm sure you will,' he agreed smoothly, and stood up.

Davina followed suit, and linked her arm with his. 'Now, let me tell you about the people you'll be meeting tonight.'

Davina chatted about her friends for most of the meal, thus managing to exclude Susan completely from the conversation. I might as well not be here, she thought, but was irritated more with Gregg than the girl. Her resentment at Susan's intrusion of their tête-à-tête luncheon was understandable, and she probably didn't realise it was Gregg who had suggested it.

Tired of being ignored, she excused herself before coffee was served.

'I don't know what time I'll be back,' she said. 'Perhaps I'd better have a key.'

'I thought of that,' Davina answered. 'You'll find one on the hall table nearest the front door.'

Susan stayed at her parents' house until after supper, then visited a girl friend who lived in the next village, and by the time she returned to Brocklehurst it was nearly one o'clock. There were no cars in the driveway, so it was obvious the guests had departed.

Were Gregg and Davina in bed? she wondered, and did not have long to wait for the answer. For as she turned the corner, at the end of the Long Gallery that led to her bedroom, she saw Davina. A vision of loveliness in diaphanous pink negligee, she glided along the corridor and stopped outside Gregg's door.

'Have a good time?' she asked as Susan drew level.

'Very,' Susan answered briefly.

'I thought I'd just make sure Gregg had everything he needed,' Davina said.

Susan's eyes swept the girl from top to toe. 'If he hasn't, I'm sure he soon will have,' she commented sweetly, and turning, entered her own room. A few seconds later she heard the door opposite open, and then swiftly close.

So much for Davina keeping a little something in reserve, Susan thought cattily. Seemingly there was nothing the girl wouldn't do to keep Brocklehurst in her possession. She didn't blame Gregg. He was no better than she had expected; a good-for-nothing womaniser, who could easily turn to one woman if he couldn't have another, and he preferably liked to have two at the time. Look at the way he had made a play for her, even though it was quite obvious Davina was warming his bed.

Susan wondered if he was seriously contemplating

marriage to Davina. His announcement that he intended to spend the summer months at Brocklehurst would certainly seem to suggest it. And the girl was perfectly suited to act the part of chatelaine. A marriage of convenience would not daunt Gregg; indeed it would suit him down to the ground. He could still continue to play around—discreetly, she was sure—when the fancy took him, and when it didn't, Davina would be on hand to satisfy his needs. No doubt the arrangement would suit her equally as well.

A spring wedding would be perfect. Charles would have been dead a year, so the proprieties would have been observed, and they would have plenty of time to honeymoon before the summer season started. Perhaps even now, as they lay together, satiated from lovemaking, they were planning it.

For some reason the thought disturbed her. Probably because she could not understand such a cold-blooded arrangement, or even contemplate it herself. Love and marriage were irrevocably inter-twined in her mind, and even if it meant remaining an old maid, she would never settle for less.

CHAPTER NINE

THE following day set the pattern for the next few weeks. Up at seven-thirty, a hurried breakfast, then out in the Land Rover with Ted Swift the bailiff, visiting the farmers and other tenants.

Gregg appeared tireless, and no matter how much she could—and did—criticise his personal life-style, Susan found it impossible to do other than admire the way he set about the task of familiarising himself with the workings of the estate. During her years at Maddox, Forbes and Maddox, she had met many high-powered men, but she had never met one better able to absorb facts quickly.

It was part of her job to fill him in on each family's history, so that they were something more than just another name. And his memory, as Gerry Rosen had told her, was phenomenal. Days later he would recall exactly what she had told him about a particular person, where they lived and what they did. She had always admired his quick wit, but not known it could be warm and gentle, until he displayed it as such during his conversations with the tenants, who, in true American style, he immediately addressed by their first names. They in their turn responded, and laughed and joked with him in easy familiarity, unusual for suspicious and wary country folk.

Nearly everyone had decided they would prefer to buy their properties, rather than lease them, and a man came down from one of the largest and most reputable estate agents in London to do the valuations. For those who were unable to obtain mortgages easily,

Gregg had offered to stand as surety for them at his bank.

'I have nothing to lose,' he had said, brushing off Susan's comment on his kindness. 'If they default, then the property reverts back to me. But I don't expect that to happen. These people are hard-working and deserve to have any help they need.'

She had been assigned one of the offices on the ground floor of the house, a small room overlooking the formal gardens at the back, and she spent most of her evenings in there, going over the leases, and dictating letters into a tape recorder, for one of the estate's secretaries to transcribe the following day.

'Do you always work at this pace?' Susan asked Gregg one morning, towards the end of the fifth week, as they tramped across the fields in the wake of the bailiff.

'Finding it difficult to keep up with me?' he smiled.

'Let's put it like this. At the end of two months it will be like a holiday going back to the office!'

He chuckled. 'You've been going at it even harder than me,' he said. 'At least I relax in the evenings.' Aware that she was breathing fast, he slowed his pace. 'I suggest you do the same.'

'I'm here to work, not play,' Susan pointed out.

'You know what they say about all work?'

'I meant I wasn't here to play with *you*, Gregg.'

'Warning me in case I get any ideas?' Blue eyes glinted at her.

'I don't think there's any "in case" about it!'

'Haven't I behaved like a perfect gentleman for the past few weeks?' he demanded with indignation—mock, she suspected.

'Only because your mind has been occupied elsewhere. I was hoping it would continue to be until I leave. Don't tell me you're getting bored with Davina already?'

'Of course not,' he assured her swiftly. 'She's very inventive.'

'Then stick with her, Gregg. I'm not.'

'*You* wouldn't have to be,' he said softly.

Fortunately Susan was saved from having to think of a cutting reply by Ted Swift, who had stopped to wait for them to catch up with him. A burly man, with a ruddy complexion, he was nearing fifty, and well liked by everyone.

'Seen enough, sir?' he asked, as they drew level. 'Or do you want to go on?'

'I thought we were going to visit Mrs Harper,' said Gregg, referring to the estate's oldest tenant, who was ninety.

'We could get to her place by backtracking a bit, and picking up the Land Rover again,' the bailiff pointed out.

'Unless Susan's tired, I'd just as soon carry on walking. It's the only way I'll ever familiarise myself with the place properly. Seeing it out of the window of the car, it doesn't really register.' Gregg turned to Susan. 'How do your legs feel?'

'I was brought up in the country,' Susan replied. 'It takes more than a few miles to tire me.'

'Do you hunt, Mr Saville?' the bailiff asked conversationally, as they carried on walking.

'Only women,' Gregg smiled. 'But sometimes *they* can be little vixens!' He gave Susan the full force of his eyes, but fortunately Ted Swift had bent down to pick up a stick to throw for his black labrador, and didn't notice.

'I know what you mean,' the bailiff chuckled, as he stood up. 'I have three teenage daughters.'

'Did you ask for a reason?' Gregg questioned.

'Yes, sir, I did. There's a meet the week after next, and I wanted to ask your permission to redirect it. Some of the hounds have been straying on to the

Wilson's farm and messing with their poultry. They're compensated, of course, but not for the mess they have to clear up.'

'You mean they cross my land?' Gregg asked.

'You're automatically Master of the Hunt,' Susan interjected, 'so they don't just cross your land, they ride right through it.'

The square jaw jutted out belligerently. 'Not any more they don't,' Gregg said. 'I have an abhorrence of blood sports, and I refuse to lend my name or land to it.'

'That won't make you very popular around these parts,' the bailiff pointed out swiftly.

'That's unfortunate,' Gregg said flatly. 'But if foxes have to be kept down—and I understand that they do—then on my land it will be carried out as humanely as possible.'

'Good for you!' said Susan.

Ted smiled briefly. 'Everyone around these parts knows *your* feelings on the matter, Susan. I remember when you tried to stop the Hunt a couple of years back.'

'Me and a hundred others,' Susan corrected. 'But they rode right through us.' She dug her hands into the pockets of her trousers to warm them, and then went on, 'What about the Hunt Ball? That's always been held at Brocklehurst.'

'Then that's another tradition I'll break with. I'll have a ball there, but it will be on behalf of the R.S.P.C.A.'

'The ballroom's going to look pretty empty with just you in it!' Susan smiled.

'If no one locally will support it, I'll fill the place with friends from London,' he replied, and what Susan had taken for a joke she now realised had not been meant as such.

They had reached a hedgerow bordering a narrow lane, across which could be seen a small stone cottage.

'That's Mrs Harper's place,' the bailiff said, as he opened the gate to let them through.

The old lady was expecting them, and after ushering them into the tiny living-room—all brass and oak, and spotlessly clean—she insisted on making them a cup of tea. It was more than welcome after their long walk, and arrived with home-made fruit cake, still warm from the oven.

'This is delicious,' Gregg commented, and held out his plate for another piece. 'It reminds me of the cake my grandmother used to bake for me when I was a boy.'

Mrs Harper's wrinkled parchment cheeks reddened with pleasure. 'Then take the rest of it back with you,' she said, and immediately rose and went into the kitchen to wrap it in tinfoil.

'You certainly said the right thing there,' Susan remarked, some half an hour later when, cake in hand, they departed.

'Well, it was delicious. But I have to confess that my maternal grandmother never went near the kitchen— she always had a cook—and my paternal grandmother died before I was born!'

'Your secret's safe with me,' Ted Swift assured him. 'She rarely has visitors, and your offer to buy her a colour television set was a real act of kindness.'

For the first time since Susan had known him, Gregg looked embarrassed. 'The Saville's have always felt it their duty to look after their tenants to the best of their ability, so Susan tells me, and that's one tradition I'm happy to carry on.'

By the time they finally returned to Brocklehurst it was nearly dark, though only five o'clock.

'How about joining me for a drink?' Gregg asked as usual.

As usual, Susan refused. 'Sorry, I have work to do.'

'Couldn't you at least vary your answer—it might

make it sound more convincing.'

'But I don't need to sound convincing,' Susan said coolly. 'I just want to make it obvious I have no desire to spend any time alone with you.'

'If you want a chaperone, then have dinner with us tonight, instead of in your office. I'll have to behave with Davina around.'

'If the Duchess isn't having guests this evening, I'm sure it's because she wants you to herself, and I wouldn't dream of intruding.'

He looked as if he were about to argue, but instead, changed the subject completely.

'I'm going to London tomorrow,' he told her. 'Fiona's husband is flying over with his lawyers to discuss some points on the Cap Ferrat development, and as it's Thursday, I've decided to stay over for the weekend.'

'Missing the bright lights?'

'Not as much as I'd anticipated,' he answered surprisingly. 'But then everything here is new to me. Perhaps after another month, I'll be glad to get back to L.A.'

'You are going back, then?'

'I have no intention of selling *Playmate*, if that's what you mean, and I'd hate to see the circulation go down because I've neglected it.' Gregg moved towards the staircase. 'Fortunately we always plan the format a few months ahead. That's why I haven't had to return sooner.'

'Are you going up to London alone?' Susan queried.

'Yes. In fact the reason I've decided to stay is because Davina is going to Scotland to a wedding. And you don't appear to want to keep me company,' he added.

'I'm sure you have plenty of numbers in your little black book to call on,' she answered tartly, and walked past him down the corridor to her office.

Gregg left early the following morning without Susan having the opportunity to see him. For once she was able to eat a leisurely breakfast—albeit on her own, as Davina always had hers in bed—and read the newspapers at the beginning of the day for a change, instead of at the end.

She had plenty of work to get on with, so the day flew by, though she had to admit it was more tedious than pleasurable, rather than the other way around when accompanying Gregg about the estate.

Davina departed on Friday afternoon—she was flying to Scotland from Birmingham—and with all the staff off for the weekend, except Danvers, Susan decided to have dinner with her parents, and then spend the night with friends, rather than on her own in the West Wing of the house.

'I'll take Lady with me,' she told Danvers. 'I've raved about her to my parents, and they keep asking me to bring her over.'

'What about tonight?' he asked, knowing she would not be returning. 'Will you fetch her back before you go to your friends?'

'No. they adore dogs, and won't mind if she sleeps with me.'

'Well, she's completely house-trained now, so you don't have to worry about that.'

It was shortly after nine when Susan drew up outside her friends' house on the outskirts of the village. She had known Jean and Martin Friar all her life, and at school, she and Jean had been inseparable.

After making a fuss of Lady, who then settled contentedly in front of the fire, they proceeded to question Susan about Gregg Saville.

'Has he improved on closer acquaintance?' Jean asked, aware of Susan's misgivings.

'I have to admit he has,' Susan replied immediately, surprising herself at having answered the question without considering it first. 'I think he's going to make a very worthy successor to Charles—in more ways than one,' she added, and proceeded to tell them about Davina.

'Well,' Jean smiled, 'she won't be very pleased to see this morning's *Globe*!' She disappeared into the kitchen, returning a few moments later carrying the paper. 'You obviously haven't seen it either.'

There was a large photograph of Gregg on the front page, accompanied by an extremely pretty woman, who looked to be in her early thirties. 'Maggie Porter', she read, 'wife of millionaire textile tycoon Bob Porter, was wined and dined last night at Les Ambassadeurs Club by ex-boy-friend and employer, Gregg Saville, who recently became the eleventh Duke of Wentworth. When asked if there was anything more to their tête-à-tête dinner than just old times sake', the ex-*Playmate* centrefold replied: 'Gregg is the only man my husband trusts me with when he's away on business.' If you believe that, folks, you'll believe anything!'

'If Davina hasn't seen it, I'm sure one of her very good friends will make sure she does,' Susan commented dryly.

'Is he really as good-looking as this?' Jean asked, indicating the picture.

'Better—and far more caring than the image he shows to the public.'

'So far you've only listed his virtues,' Martin interjected. 'How about telling us what's wrong with him?'

Surprisingly, other than his faithlessness, and uncaring attitude to women, there was little Susan could find to say. But it was a serious flaw; a shallow trait, totally lacking commitment, and showed a certain immaturity of character.

'He's only like that because he hasn't met a woman

to hold his interest,' Martin asserted. 'But when he does, he'll fall all the harder, because it will be for the first time.'

'There speaks a man with the vast experience of marrying the one and only girl-friend he ever had,' his wife teased affectionately.

Susan smiled. 'Gregg Saville's mind is on a different plane from yours, Martin, and for Jean's sake, thank heaven for it!'

'Well, it's about time you found yourself a man as wonderful as me!' Martin looked towards his wife. 'How about arranging a small party tomorrow evening and asking Tony Granger? He's just bought old man Pierson's practice over in Wiberlee,' he explained to Susan, naming a lawyer in the nearby market town.

'What a good idea,' said Jean. 'And Susan can stay the night again. You don't have to rush back for anything, do you?'

'Only work,' Susan smiled again. 'But I can easily catch up on Sunday.'

Tony Granger was a sophisticated young man, and hailed from London, but had decided to opt out of the rat race and settle for the quieter life of a country practice. Susan was interested to hear his reasons, and also enjoyed talking shop, so the evening passed pleasantly and swiftly.

'You two appeared to get on like a house on fire,' Jean commented, when the last guest had departed and they were re-hashing the evening as they cleared away the worst of the mess.

'He's very nice,' Susan said. 'But I don't think he's the one who's going to set my heart aflame.'

'Are you seeing him again?' Jean asked.

'He's taking me out for dinner tomorrow night.'

'Well, even if he isn't going to be the big romance in your life, at least a little harmless flirtation will give you something else to think about, other than

Mr Saville,' Jean commented.

Later, as she lay in bed, with Lady curled in her basket in a corner of the room, Susan thought over Jean's remark. Perhaps she had become somewhat obsessed with Gregg. Certainly she had frequently brought him into her conversation with Tony. But then, working for him as she was, surely it was only natural? But was it also natural to compare Tony to him, or every other man in the room for that matter, and find them all wanting? And not just in the looks department, as when they had first met. Now there were so many other things she could admire; his charm, his keen sense of humour, his quick mind, his adaptability, and of course, the concern he had shown for the tenants since taking over the estate.

She closed her eyes, and an image of Gregg came so clearly into mind that it was as if a cameo had been painted on her eyeballs. She gave a shiver, and sat up again. The impossible, the dreaded had happened. She had fallen in love with Gregg. What she had seen as a purely physical attraction was far more—and had she not been so blinded by fear of giving way to it, she would have recognised the fact a long time ago.

What a hopeless situation! Although Gregg desired her very much, and had a certain admiration for her intelligence and humour, he would never be satisfied with one woman after the constant excitement of so many love-affairs. And unlike Davina, she had made it quite clear she wanted total commitment in a relationship.

He must never realise how she felt, for she had no doubt he would exploit it to wear down her resistance, and were she to submit, though she might hold his interest a little longer than most, he would still discard her in the end. Yet now she was aware of her love for him, how could she bear to be near him, knowing he was in the arms of Davina, or some other woman?

Tired and listless after a night spent tossing and turning, she made her way down to breakfast the following morning. But if her friends noticed the dark circles under her eyes they made no comment, and appeared all the brighter in contrast to herself.

She left soon afterwards, determined to put in a full day's work, more to keep her mind off Gregg than from necessity, and to that end, she succeeded. She did not even stop for lunch, making do with a pot of coffee, so that by the time Tony called for her she was pleased to see him, if for no other reason than the fact that she was exceedingly hungry.

But that was unfair to the man. For he was intelligent, and kind, and after a delicious meal at the village pub, when he asked to see her again, she agreed.

He kissed her briefly on the mouth when he said goodnight, and relieved he had not tried to go further, Susan made her way into the house.

Surprisingly, the hall was a blaze of lights, as it was when Davina and Gregg were in residence. But Davina, she knew, would not be returning until Tuesday, and it was unlikely Gregg would wish to leave the bed of his old flame to return to an empty one.

But in this she was wrong. For as she turned the handle of her bedroom door, his opened, and he stepped out.

He was in a fine temper. It was apparent in the set of his shoulders and mouth, and the glitter in his eyes as they swept over her, taking in her hair, which was dishevelled from the strong breeze that had whipped it as she stepped out of the car. But as he spoke, it became apparent he assumed it to be for an entirely different reason.

'I saw your boy-friend bring you home. Have a nice weekend with him?'

'Not that it's any of your business, but I didn't spend the weekend with him. We only met yesterday.'

'Who did you spend Friday night with then? Someone else?' he asked, making her wish she had phrased her reply differently. He came towards her, and she backed away from him into her room. 'I telephoned early on Saturday,' he went on, 'to see if you would have dinner with me if I returned. But Dawson told me you weren't expected back until this morning.'

'What happened to Maggie Porter?' retorted Susan. 'Tired of her, or the other way around?'

'How typical of you to believe the worst, instead of the truth—which is exactly as Maggie was quoted. Bob Porter is a friend of mine, and I don't go to bed with my friend's wives.'

'My, my, how honourable you are, Gregg! If only I'd realised it, I might have given in to you myself,' she mocked.

'Well, it's not too late,' he grated, and came into her room, closing the door behind him.

'Get out,' she ordered. '*Get out*!'

'Not until I've had what you're willing to give everyone else,' he snapped, catching her by the arm and pulling her against him.

Her heart began to pound furiously, and for the first time with him, she felt fear.

'That's not true!' she cried, and tried to pull free of him. But that was the worst thing she could have done, for it only served to arouse him further.

His grip tightened, and he pressed her close against him, so that she could feel the hardness of his thighs, and the steel-like quality of his chest.

'You've played cat and mouse with me for weeks,' he said thickly. 'But now the game is over.'

His nearness, and his breath, warm on her ears, were making it increasingly difficult for her to think clearly.

'Please,' she begged. 'Please, Gregg——'

'That's just what I aim to do, my beautiful Susan,' he murmured, and moved his hands across her shoulders and down her back, twining his arms about her as if he was trying to mould her into him and fuse their bodies.

It was madness, but her longing for him was so great that even though she knew their lovemaking would have nothing to do with the word love—on his side at least—she no longer cared or thought about tomorrow, and the days, weeks and months after that, when remembering his arms about her would be a torment.

It was tonight, it was now, and that was all that mattered.

Slowly she lifted her head, and their eyes met and held. The softening of Gregg's features and half-parted lips were a sign that he had understood her acquiescence, and he bent until his mouth rested on hers. There was no hesitation, no questioning in his touch. He wanted her, and she was offering no resistance; he was master of the situation in every way.

'Susan, Susan,' he whispered, as he kissed her, demanding more and more with his lips, while his body, hardening as he rubbed against her, made her aware of the full extent of his desire.

With the ease of long practice, his hand reached for the zip of her dress, and in one sure movement pulled it down and over the curve of her hips, so that it lay in a soft heap around her feet.

She wore nothing beneath the top of it, and only lacy bikini panties beneath her tights, and she instinctively moved her arms to cover herself.

'I do believe you're shy,' Gregg murmured, and stepped away from her so that he could look into her face. 'You are. I can see it in your eyes, and in the way your lashes are trembling.'

Her lids quivered, and with his right hand he touched the soft curve of her cheek, tracing its delicate line back to the lobe of her ear, and then down the side of her slender neck. 'My swan, my beautiful golden swan,' he continued, in a voice deeper than ever. 'There's a little pulse beating in your throat. How fast it's going . . . Are you frightened of me too, Susan?'

Still keeping her eyes lowered, she gave a slight, negative shake of her head.

'Then why don't you take your arms away, and look at me?'

With an effort she did, staring at him in silence, hoping he would not notice her hands, clenched to stop them from shaking. How intent his eyes were, the irises enlarged with passion.

'That's better,' he said softly, then pulling her close again, moved both hands beneath her knees and swung her off her feet. He carried her across the room to the four-poster, placing her gently on the soft mattress, then looked at her once again, breath quickening, eyes slumbrous, before switching on the bedside light and moving over to the door to turn off the centre one.

Swift fingers undid the buttons of his shirt, the buckle of his belt. Then there was the rustle of his jeans, before he lowered himself down beside her and gathered her into his arms.

Naked flesh on naked flesh, warm, sensual, instantly arousing Gregg moved his chest gently against her breasts, teasing, rubbing, pressing before his mouth came to claim the sweet pink tips, until Susan felt herself roused to a fever pitch of need; need to run her hands through the thick blond hair that curled at the nape of his neck; rake her fingers down his back and along the firm flesh, to the tautly rounded buttocks; press herself closer and closer to him, until they became one.

'You're beautiful,' he murmured, 'so beautiful,' and

he lifted himself slightly away from her in order to gaze into her face, and then down the length of her body, with a tenderness she had never thought to see in him. 'Every single part of you, my darling, was made for love. We're going to be perfect together.'

His hands moved under the waist of her tights, to ease them gently over the soft swell of her stomach, down over the curve of her hips, until the tips of his fingers reached the top of her panties. But as he was about to touch and plunder the softness beneath, there was a loud knocking on his bedroom door, and the voice of Dawson could be heard.

'Mr Saville!' he called, and then when there was no reply, his voice grew louder. 'Mr Saville, sir, it's an emergency. It's Lady!'

'Oh, God!' Gregg swore as he moved away from her and swung long legs on to the floor. 'What timing!'

Susan felt an almost hysterical urge to giggle. No doubt nerves and the pent-up emotion of passion unassuaged partly accounted for it, but she could not help seeing the funny side of the situation as well.

'I'm glad *you* think it's funny,' Gregg fumed, as the laughter she could no longer contain burst forth. But watching him struggle with the zip of his jeans, after first putting his shirt on inside out, reminded her of a Whitehall farce.

'Leave Dawson to me,' she instructed calmly, and ran into the bathroom, her near-nakedness no embarrassment now. Hurriedly she splashed water on her feet, neck and hands, put on her towelling robe, and, dripping wet, dashed to the door.

'What's wrong?' she asked, heart pounding, but sounding composed. 'Can I be of any help?'

'It's Lady.' The butler turned, and for the first time Susan could remember, looked flustered. 'Something's caught in her throat, and she appears to be having difficulty breathing. I've phoned for Mr Simpson,' he said, naming the vet, 'and he'll be over in a few minutes. But I thought I'd better let Mr Saville know.'

'I saw him about ten minutes ago, before I got into my bath.' Superstitious, Susan crossed her fingers as she spoke. 'He was about to take a turn in the garden—Too much brandy, he said,' she improvised hurriedly, and hoped it sounded a logical enough reason for a sane man to go out in the freezing cold at twelve o'clock at night.

'Do you think you could get dressed and find him?' Dawson asked, appearing to accept it without question. 'I don't want to leave the poor little mite alone any longer.'

He hurried away, and Susan closed her bedroom door again.

'That was quick thinking.' Gregg's voice was no longer angry, but admiring. 'One could almost think you'd had some practice.'

'I hope that was meant as a joke, because if not, I find the implication disgusting!'

'It was.' He smiled apologetically. 'And in pretty poor taste too. Put it down to frustration and concern for Lady.' He took a swift look at himself in the cheval mirror. 'I'd better wait for you to get dressed. It might look rather odd if we don't appear together.'

The emergency was dealt with swiftly and efficiently by the vet, who put his fingers down the puppy's throat and extracted a tiny piece of splintered bone.

'Lamb,' he said, holding it up. 'What fool gave her that?'

'One of the maids, I expect,' Dawson answered.

'Well, you'd better tell all the staff, and make sure it doesn't happen again. We're very lucky it didn't completely block her windpipe. She looks a bit down in the mouth,' Gregg said appropriately. 'Perhaps she ought to sleep with me tonight.'

'There's no need, Mr Saville,' Dawson interposed. 'I'm quite happy to have her in my room—in fact I was going to suggest it.'

'He's a real softie,' Gregg remarked to Susan as they left the kitchen quarters. 'And I have to admit I'm relieved he took Lady off my hands. As fond as I am of her, I'd much rather be with you. Now we can start where we left off.'

'Quite the contrary, Gregg. We'll start where we began. With me saying no.'

He threw her a puzzled look. 'But——'

'But nothing,' Susan interrupted coolly. 'I told you when we first met I didn't go in for casual liaisons, and that still applies.'

'Don't tell me you weren't enjoying yourself.'

'There wouldn't be much point, considering the position I was in when we were interrupted,' she commented dryly. 'But I didn't come to you, Gregg. You forced yourself on me, and. . . .' She shrugged. 'Well, I've never denied I find you attractive.'

'I'm sorry for the way I behaved,' he apologised gruffly. 'But I've wanted you from the first moment I saw you in the saloon at Eureka, and having you so near these last few weeks, and yet so distant, was driving me mad.'

'What drove you into Davina's arms?' she asked scathingly. 'Consolation?'

'You know nothing of my relationship with her,' Gregg said angrily. 'You only think you do.'

'I'm not interested in hearing about it either.'

They had reached the Long Gallery, and he stopped in front of a portrait of the fifth Duke, elegantly attired in silk and lace; a stark contrast to the present title-holder's denim. But only in the way they were dressed. The determined features were the same, as were the bright blue eyes. But however determinedly they were looking at her now, intent on persuading her back into bed, Susan was equally determined not to give way. Fortuitously brought to her senses, she had no intention of losing them again.

'Why do you always think the worst of me?' Gregg burst out.

'Have you ever given me cause to think otherwise?'

He gave her a long intent stare. 'What would you like me to do?'

'Find the answer for yourself, Gregg. It's about time you did some soul-searching.'

'Is it hearts and flowers you're after . . .!'

'There wouldn't be much point with you,' she said scornfully. 'You haven't got a heart.'

'Let me prove I have where you're concerned. Come back to the States with me, Susan.'

'How long for?' she asked. 'A week . . . a month . . . until a new face takes your fancy? Until I bore you like all the others?'

He shook his head. 'You're not like all the others,' he said huskily. 'You amuse me, irritate me, intrigue me, tantalise me until I can't think straight.' He reached out for her hand and pulled her nearer to him. 'But bore me—never.'

'You say that now, because you want me. You'd say anything to get what you want.'

'That's not true. I've never pretended with a woman. My girl-friends have always known exactly where they stand. And you stand far and above them all. I'm crazy about you—so much so that I can't concentrate on anything, or anyone else.' He drew her fingers to his mouth and gently kissed them. 'Tell me you feel something for me too, Susan.'

Abruptly she pulled her hand away, seeing his words as nothing but a ploy to persuade her to have an affair with him.

'Why, Gregg? Does your ego need feeding? Do women normally have to spell out why they want to go to bed with you?'

'No, they don't. But *you* do.' He looked at her, his eyes puzzled. 'Dammit, you must feel something for me,' he insisted. 'If we hadn't been interrupted this time, you'd have allowed me to make love to you properly.'

'I thought I'd already made the reason for that clear,' she said matter-of-factly. 'I find you physically attractive, and I was feeling sexy.'

'Didn't your weekend satisfy you?'

'Did your weekend satisfy *you*?' she responded swiftly.

To her astonishment a wave of red flooded his face.

'It's different for a man,' he said sharply.

Susan forced herself to laugh. 'Your ideas are rather antiquated, aren't they? Things have changed since Victorian days, Gregg. Or hadn't you realised it?'

'Only with a certain type—and you're not one of them.'

'A minute ago you insinuated the opposite.'

'I don't know what I'm saying,' he said roughly. 'Don't you know what you've done to me?'

'Nothing—apart from making you realise you're not irresistible,' Susan said flippantly.

'For God's sake be serious,' he snapped.

'About us? That's a joke.'

'Is it?' he asked flatly. 'I don't happen to think so.'

'But Davina might.'

'*Davina*?' he questioned forcefully. 'What the hell has she to do with the way I feel about you?'

At last the control she had been exercising snapped. 'You are without doubt the most unprincipled bastard I've ever met!' she almost shouted.

'And you are without doubt the most puzzling girl *I've* ever met.' There was frustration in his voice. 'I just don't understand what you want.'

'And you never will, Gregg!'

Anticipating the hand that reached out to detain her, Susan sidestepped it and ran down the Long Gallery to the corridor that led to her bedroom.

She wondered if he would follow her, but all she heard was silence. Perhaps he had decided on a drink to help drown his disappointment. Certainly he must be cursing Fate, in the shape of Lady, for her untimely intervention.

She slipped off her dress and went into the bathroom. The smell of Gregg's after-shave still lingered on her skin, the touch of his hands too, reminding her of the pleasures they might have shared, the heights the could have reached, if only he had said he loved her. For she suspected that he did, and either could not, or would not admit it to himself. What else could it mean when he had told her she meant more to him than any other woman he had known?

Yet in spite of that, at no time had he intimated that he saw himself as anything other than her lover. Perhaps, like Charles, when it came to choosing a wife, only the best pedigree was good enough.

CHAPTER TEN

SUSAN was not the sort of girl to give up something she wanted without a fight, and a future with Gregg, a chance to share his life, to bear his children, to give him all the love he would ever need, was something she wanted above all else.

Armed with the knowledge that she meant more to him than just another conquest—and possibly loved her—she determined to build on it, in the hope that he would be forced to recognise and admit it. She still had another three weeks at Brocklehurst before her work was completed; three weeks to strengthen the feelings she had already aroused in him—not the obvious one of desire, for that had no need of strengthening, but ones that were of equal importance to a permanent relationship; affection, shared interests and humour, and companionship.

If at the end of that period Gregg still only saw her in terms of an affair, then however painful the parting, she would be forced to accept that they could have no future together.

When Gregg joined her at breakfast, he looked as if he too had spent a sleepless night. His eyes were shadowed, and he complained of a headache. But he made no reference to the previous evening—possibly because there were staff hovering about—and teased and flirted with her in his usual manner. Taking her cue from him, Susan also carried on as if nothing had happened.

'Do you need me to go with you and Ted today, or can I stay here and concentrate on the contracts?' she asked, helping herself to a large dollop of home-made marmalade.

'As it's pouring, I'll let you off,' he smiled. 'But if it clears up this afternoon, how about coming for a ride with me? It's about time I sat on a horse, and showed the locals that though I'm a Yank, I don't lack all the social graces!'

'I'll have to go down to my parents' to collect my riding gear,' she replied. 'But I'll wait and see if it stops first.'

'Get it anyway,' he instructed. 'If we can't go out today, we'll make it tomorrow.

Fortuitously the rain did stop, and though the skies were still heavy, Susan agreed to accompany him. There were a dozen horses to choose from in the stables, and she picked a chestnut gelding who, the stableboy assured her, was sweet and docile.

'How well do you ride, sir?' the lad asked Gregg, eyeing his unconventional outfit of jeans and heavy sweater.

'Competently rather than Olympic standard,' he smiled.

'Then I suggest you try Rob Roy.' The lad indicated a sturdy bay. 'He's got plenty of get up and go if you want it, but he's just as happy at a trot.'

They rode for several miles without speaking, and as the sun peaked through the clouds, by mutual consent, drew to a stop by the lake. Gregg jumped down, helped Susan to the ground, and then tethered the horses to a tree and left them to graze.

'How about a nip of brandy to help the circulation?' he asked, removing a thin silver flask from beneath his sweater.

'No, thanks. I hate the stuff—it tastes like medicine.' Idly she picked up a stone and sent it skimming across the water. 'You ride very well, Gregg. Did you learn as a child?'

'At prep school. I even managed a few jumps then.'

He picked up a stone himself, and made a successful attempt to beat her throw, watching until the last ripple had disappeared before continuing. 'It was the only thing I did like about being sent away to school. It's a barbaric custom, putting children in the care of strangers during their formative years—for any period of their lives, come to that. Parents abdicate their responsibility, and then wonder why their offspring aren't closer to them.'

'But you're close to your mother—it doesn't seem to have affected your relationship adversely,' she commented.

'Because she had a good reason for doing it. She wasn't selfishly shirking her responsibility. She realised that bringing me up in a household of women would have been far worse for me. As it was, I was spoiled rotten during the holidays.'

'And women have gone on spoiling you ever since,' Susan said dryly.

'Except for you. You seem able to resist my charms.'

'Perhaps if you're lucky enough to catch me at the right moment again, I won't be able to,' she said lightly.

'Is that an invitation?' he asked softly.

'Don't try to find out by putting it to the test, Gregg. You might find yourself taking a cold bath.' She indicated the lake. 'Though come to think of it, it might be just what you need!'

'It would only dampen my ardour temporarily. Five minutes later I'd be ready to try again.'

'In that case, I'd better make sure I'm never alone with you,' she smiled. 'Fighting you off all the time is becoming a bit of a bore.'

He gave her a slow studied look. 'If I weren't convinced you didn't really want to keep fighting me, I wouldn't keep up the attack.'

'With so many others to choose from, why keep bothering with me?'

'I thought I'd made that quite clear to you last night.' He took another swig of brandy, and gulped it down thirstily, as if needing Dutch courage for what he had to say. 'You—you're ruining my life,' he said jerkily. 'You've wormed your way into my system so that I'm no good with any other woman. These last few weeks I've lived like a monk. *Me!*' His voice was full of disgust. 'Before I met you, I could make love three or four times a night—now even kissing anyone but you is an effort.'

He looked so tense, so uncertain, so unlike the devil-may-care man she had grown to love, that she longed to touch him, to reassure him. But that would be dangerous, because he would see it as a sign of weakening on her part, and until he was willing to admit that what he really felt for her was love, and not just desire, she had to hold her emotions in check.

'I'm very sorry, Gregg,' she said flatly, 'but you'll have to solve your problem yourself. I have no intention of having an affair with you.'

She felt his hand on her arm, his fingers digging tightly into her, as he pulled her closer. 'What the hell will you settle for, then?' he asked violently. 'Marriage? Is that why you're holding out on me? Because you couldn't hook Charles by giving him what he wanted, do you think by refusing me you'll provoke me enough to make you a duchess?' His eyes showed his anger. There were deep creases from his brow to his nose and his lower lip was sucked in. 'Oh yes,' he went on, misinterpreting the look of astonishment his accusation had brought to her face. 'Davina told me *all* about you and Charles.'

'And you believed her?' Susan's voice was quiet, but full of contempt. 'You really believe that's the sort of girl I am . . . That that's the reason I refused to let you

. . . My God, and to think I——'

It was impossible to continue. The tears that had been threatening, were choking her. She wrenched herself from his grip and ran towards the horses. Hurriedly she pulled the reins free and mounted—not her own plodding chestnut gelding this time, but Gregg's much faster bay. She wanted to get away from him, as far away as possible, and had no intention of allowing him the chance to catch her.

She heard him call her name, but did not even turn her head. Instead she dug her heels into the horse's flanks and urged him into a canter.

On and on she rode, not looking or caring in which direction she was riding, as long as she was distancing herself from Gregg. The tears flowed freely now; tears for what might have been, but was now just an empty dream. If he had had any real feelings for her, he would never have believed Davina's lies. God, what a fool she had been to imagine he had fallen in love with her! All that had happened was that her refusal to give in to him had turned into such an obsession, it had made him impotent, so that he was willing to say anything, offer anything—but love and marriage, of course—to possess her, in the hope it would cure him.

Well, as far as she was concerned, he could stay impotent for the rest of his life. Come what may, she would leave Brocklehurst, even if it meant facing Mr Maddox's wrath. She had done the bulk of the work, and someone else could easily finish it.

It had started to drizzle, but she did not even notice it; did not notice the fallen tree either until it was too late to pull the horse up. He shied abruptly to one side to avoid it, so that she was at one angle and he another. She made a desperate attempt to hold on to the reins, but the force of the movement was too great, and losing her grip on his flanks, she went somersaulting over his head.

Instinctively she flung one hand against her breast, the other up to protect her face. But it was to no avail. A knotted tangle of root hit her hard on the temple and a jagged scar of light flashed across her eyes before everything went black.

Her next recollection was of a white cloud coming down towards her, while she stared at it helplessly, powerless to move and praying it would stop before it enveloped her completely. But it remained hovering above her head, and only as she continued to stare at it did she realise it wasn't a cloud but a ceiling. As this thought came into her mind so total reality returned, though not her memory.

'Where am I?' she gasped, and went to sit up.

'Lie still,' her mother's voice said. 'You're in hospital and perfectly safe.'

'Hospital?' Susan croaked.

'In Wiberlee,' her mother said.

'Wiberlee?' How did I get here?'

'Gregg—Mr Saville brought you. You've been here for four days, darling.'

Susan looked in the direction of the voice. It was surprisingly difficult to focus, but gradually the face she loved took shape; a pale triangle with soft blonde hair, tinged with grey. 'Mummy,' she said huskily, and cleared her throat to speak more easily, but her voice remained a bare thread of sound.

'Don't try to speak, sweetheart. You've plenty of time for that.'

'I must ... I must know what's wrong with me. Why do I feel so awful?'

'You've had concussion and pneumonia. You were lying for hours on the wet earth before Gregg and the search party found you.'

'I can't remember that—only falling.'

'You're very lucky your riding hat stayed firmly on

your head, or you might have been killed,' her mother told her.

'I feel half dead now.' Susan struggled to sit up, but could not command her body to do as she wished. Even the effort of trying to move made her feel nauseous, and the room spun alarmingly.

Her mother reached out, and put a reassuring hand on Susan's shoulder.

'Your hand's cold,' Susan protested.

'Only because you're very hot.' Mrs Andrews took her hand away. 'The doctor should be here any moment. He comes in twice a day.'

No sooner had she spoken than the door opened, and a tall, thin figure came to stand beside her.

'Well, Susan, this is a nice surprise. How are you feeling?'

'Terrible.' She forced a smile to her lips.

'Another few days and you'll be up and about quite normally,' he said cheerfully. 'Now let me take a look at you, if I may. Just lie back and relax.'

Susan would have found it impossible to do anything else, and she kept her eyes closed, aware of the doctor's hands on her body and the hard cold edge of a stethoscope. She was asked to move on to her side, and then after what seemed an interminable length of time was told to lie flat again. By this time it was an effort to keep her eyes open, and she heard the doctor's voice coming from a long way off as he told her there was nothing to worry about now, and reiterating that she would soon be better.

'There's no need to put her back in the oxygen tent,' the doctor instructed the nurse hovering behind him. 'We'll just keep her on the antibiotics.'

'If you'd like to go and have a coffee, Mrs Andrews,' the nurse said, as the doctor left, 'I'll give your daughter a nice refreshing bed-bath.'

Her mother pressed Susan's hand. 'I'll telephone

Daddy and tell him the good news that you're fully conscious.'

'Now, young lady, let me see about making you more comfortable.' The nurse's voice was as calm as her hands, which were passing a warm flannel over Susan's face, before removing her nightdress. 'Off with the old, and on with the new,' she said. 'My, what pretty things Mr Saville bought for you! And ribbons to match for your hair too. He had them sent down from London—Janet Reger,' she chattered on. 'They must have cost a pretty penny, I'm sure.'

Barely absorbing what she had said, Susan submitted to her ministrations, surprised to find she felt better for them. 'What time is it?' she asked.

'You're always asking the time—even though you've only been half conscious,' the nurse told her with a smile. 'And as soon as I tell you, you forget.'

'I won't forget now.'

'No, dear, I'm sure you won't. You're a different girl today.' The woman showed Susan her watch, which indicated eleven. 'You're well on the road to recovery.'

'It's a steep road,' Susan whispered. 'I hope I have the strength to climb it.'

'Now stop feeling sorry for yourself,' the nurse said briskly, fluffing her pillows. 'You'll be up and about in no time—didn't you hear the doctor say so?'

'Yes, but——'

'There are no buts,' came the firm reassurance. 'Now, how about a nice cup of broth? It's the best way of getting back your strength.'

Before Susan could refuse, the nurse disappeared, returning a few minutes later with a steaming bowl. She forced several spoonfuls of it down Susan's reluctant throat, then beamed happily. 'Mr Saville left a message to phone him as soon as you'd recovered enough for visitors. How about my letting him know you have, and asking him to call in this afternoon?'

'I don't want to see him,' Susan said forcefully, surprising the nurse, who stepped back a pace to look at her.

'You don't mean that, Miss Andrews. He's been so concerned for you. The first night when you were so ill, he stayed at your bedside with your parents, and he's phoned or popped in every day since. And look at all these beautiful flowers. They're nearly all from him, and they're changed every other day.'

For the first time Susan took in her surroundings properly. Indeed the room was filled with flowers; baskets, bowls and vases, overflowing in such a profusion of colour and dewy perfection, they looked like an advertisement for Moyses Stevens.

'Give them to the wards—I don't want them in here,' she instructed and closed her eyes to their beauty.

'Now, that's being silly.' The nurse's tone was one she no doubt used to admonish difficult children. 'He'll be most upset.'

'Then don't tell him. Just get rid of them, please.'

Tut-tutting, the woman did as she was told, leaving just a vase filled with roses from Susan's parents, and a bowl of green plants from the office. 'You've had many more from your friends, but they've died in the warmth from the central heating,' the nurse informed her as she departed.

As I nearly did, Susan thought when she was alone. No doubt Gregg blamed himself for her accident, and guilt was the cause of his concern and generosity. It extended to the private room in the hospital too, she learned from her mother, as well as the day and night nurses she had had until it was certain she was out of danger.

By the following evening she was feeling so much better that the doctor told her she could get up for a short time the next day. But when she did, she was surprised at how shaky she felt, and quickly grew tired, even though she did little but walk around the room examining her cards from well-wishers. But each day brought a slight improvement, and by the end of the week she was almost back to her old self.

She did not look fit, though, for she had lost a good deal of weight. Her collarbones protruded sharply and the thinness of her body made her breasts look fuller. Some men would prefer her this way, she mused, as she studied her reflection in the bathroom mirror. But Gregg had liked slenderness with soft curves. Gregg again. In spite of everything, how difficult it was to stop thinking about him, and wondering where he was and what he was doing.

But that problem at least was solved at the weekend by her mother.

'He's left for America—to spend Christmas with his family, it said in the papers. Look, darling, there's a picture of him here in the *Mail*.'

Studying his handsome, smiling face, and the tall lithe body, towering over Davina, her arm linked intimately in his as they posed on the steps of the plane, Susan almost hated him. So much for his concern! Instead of waiting and hoping she would change her mind and see him, he had rushed back to the States. But then why should he wait and hope? she rebuked herself. He did not love her, and if she had needed any further evidence, it was here, in the gossip columns.

'You've fallen for him, haven't you?' her mother asked. 'It's written all over your face.' Susan nodded, unable to bring herself to speak. 'Why didn't you agree to see him, then?' Mrs Andrews continued. 'He was like a man demented when you were first brought in here, and I'm sure it was more than just concern because you were working for him.'

'Conscience,' Susan said flatly, and when she was able to swallow the lump in her throat, she told her mother the whole story. 'But he only ever saw me in terms of another affair,' she ended, 'and when I turned him down, he accused me of wanting to trap him into marriage for his title.'

'People often say things they don't mean when they're angry,' her mother pointed out dispassionately. 'Perhaps if you'd seen him and given him a chance to——'

'He'll never change. If he does marry, it will be Davina. He as good as told me so weeks ago.'

Her mother looked surprised, but made no further mention of him, except to tell her that Gregg had insisted she recuperate at Brocklehurst.

'I wanted to find other accommodation for Herr München and his wife,' said Mrs Andrews, referring to her paying guests, 'but Gregg wouldn't hear of it. And really it seems a sensible idea, with all the staff sitting there doing nothing.'

Realising she was not strong enough to go back to her flat and fend for herself, Susan reluctantly agreed.

Brocklehurst seemed strangely empty, and somehow sad, a mirror image of how she herself felt inside. Walking across the fields, and on the lawns, with Lady—whom Gregg had decided not to take back as a companion for his bitch in Los Angeles, but to keep as a pet at Brocklehurst—Susan was constantly reminded of him, and the few happy weeks they had spent together.

It was a relief to finally leave and return to London. At least she was not continually recalling memories of him there. For she was not going to pine for him for ever. She would live her life to the full, and hope that one day she would have forgotten him sufficiently to be able to put someone else in his place. The thought was a bitter one, for the only place Gregg had ever occupied in her life had been in her mind, though her desire for him had always been so strong that imagination had banished reality, and she had been able to make herself believe that when she was held in his arms, caressed by his hands, and warmed by his words, it had meant something more to him.

CHAPTER ELEVEN

SEEMING to sense that she needed to keep her mind fully occupied, Stanley Maddox ensured Susan had a heavy work-load. She absorbed herself in it, even at weekends, until the pain she felt became merely a dull ache, and she was able to resume her social life and start dating other men.

Christmas was spent with her parents, as Herr München and his wife had returned to Germany for the holidays. Tony Granger took her out a few times over the ten-day period, and even came up to London to see her afterwards. But when she made it perfectly clear that she was not prepared to give him exclusive rights on her time, he faded from the scene.

For the first time she accepted an invitation from a client—before Gregg, she had preferred not to mix business with pleasure—the son of the owner of one of Britain's largest breweries. He introduced her into a completely different social circle, where a new, pretty face was always welcome, and she was kept busy every night; theatres, restaurants, discos, exclusive clubs. She even found her name linked romantically in the gossip columns with two millionaires she had only met briefly at a party.

'You're looking too thin, my dear,' Stanley Maddox commented at the end of February. 'You can't burn the candle at both ends—you'll have a breakdown.'

'If you have any complaints about my work——' she began stiffly, immediately on the defensive, as she was so often these days.

'Of course not. You're too diligent, that's the trouble. You should have gone away to the sun after your accident. It would have done you more good than recuperating in that huge, draughty house.'

'I didn't fancy going away on my own,' Susan answered truthfully.

'You should find yourself a nice young man to take you. A husband,' he added hurriedly, in case she had misunderstood. 'I had hoped you and Jonathan——'

They were interrupted by the entrance of his secretary, with some letters for him to sign, and Susan took the opportunity to excuse herself and leave.

Gregg was scheduled to return early in March, in time to finalise the arrangements for the ball he planned to hold at Brocklehurst. The proceeds were to be shared between the R.S.P.C.A. and the Save the Children Fund. He had cleverly combined the two, so that those of his neighbours who might have been offended by the first—seeing his support of the R.S.P.C.A. as rubbing salt in the wound of his refusal to hold the Hunt Ball at his house—would feel churlish at refusing to support the children's charity.

To her surprise, Susan received a complimentary ticket, as did all the senior members of the staff of the law firm. The dance was to be held on the last Saturday of the month, and everyone was invited to spend the night at the house.

Susan's first reaction was to refuse, but when, shortly before Gregg was due back in England, she saw in the papers that he had sold *Playmate* and the reason for it, she decided to accept, and prove to herself, once and for all, that she had got him completely out of her system.

'Questioned on the reason for the sale of his magazine,' she read, 'Mr Saville (he has officially dropped the title of Duke of Wentworth) answered: 'I'm in love, and intend to marry, and owning a magazine like *Playmate* is not an occupation for a married man. I intend to spend part of my time at

Brocklehurst, which as you know is going to be used as a hotel during the summer months, and the remainder in the States, where I'm launching a current affairs magazine. I'm afraid I'm not cut out to be a full-time duke!'

Asked who the lucky girl was going to be, he had smiled enigmatically, and refused to comment. 'But it is no secret,' the article went on, 'that since inheriting the title he has been the constant companion of his late cousin's wife, Davina, Duchess of Wentworth, daughter of millionaire banker Freddie Harcourt Tyler.'

Susan had recently had a hefty rise, and decided to blow some of it on a dress suitable for the occasion. She would probably never have the opportunity of wearing it again, but what the hell! When Gregg announced his engagement, as she suspected he would, at the ball, she was determined to appear at her best, so that when he looked at her, he would still lust for her, and regret she was lost to him for ever.

She had her hair re-styled too, going to a hairdresser who was the current darling of the smart set. Luckily he was not scissors-happy, but cut and shaped her hair into the nape of her neck, and then swept it softly back from her face and over the tips of her ears. It was youthful, yet sophisticated, and she liked it immediately, as did everyone else.

The guest list had caused a good deal of comment in the press, for there was no doubt it was going to be one of the social events of the year. Famous names from all walks of life would be attending, and Gregg had hired a train, complete with dining car serving champagne, and coaches to collect and return the guests to Wiberlee station.

'It must be costing him a packet,' Jonathan remarked, when he collected Susan on the day. He had offered to drive her, and she had accepted. He was still keen to resume their relationship, but though she consistently refused, they remained on friendly terms. 'He might as well have donated twenty thousand or so to the charities, and saved himself a headache.'

'I've no doubt the Duchess helped organise it,' Susan said. 'And when money is no object, nothing is a headache!'

It was a sour comment, but then she did not feel in a sweet mood. For all her outward show of bravado, deep down inside, she dreaded seeing Gregg again. Dreaded it because she knew she loved him still; would always love him, no matter what.

He was not there to greet them when they arrived. Busy with the caterers, Dawson apologised on his behalf, before showing Susan up to the room she had previously occupied.

'May I get you some tea or coffee, or something stronger?' the butler enquired.

'Coffee would be lovely,' Susan smiled. 'And do you think you could manage a couple of biscuits too? I didn't have any lunch, and I'm ravenous.'

Dawson did even better, for when he returned with a pot of coffee, he also brought up a plate of smoked salmon sandwiches.

The condemned woman ate a hearty meal, Susan thought to herself, as she tucked into them. Perhaps it was nerves that had given her this empty feeling in the pit of her stomach. Certainly it had not disappeared even when she had consumed the lot.

With several hours to go, she decided on a leisurely bath to help pass the time. She had not packed her dress, merely laid it over the back seat of Jonathan's car in its plastic bag, so she had only needed to bring a small overnight case for the rest of her things.

Laying out her nightdress on the bed, she remembered the ones Gregg had bought her when she had been in hospital. Like his flowers, she had given them away, though not to the patients this time, but to the nurses who had looked after her. She sighed. If only she had been able to rid herself of the memory of him quite so easily!

The ball was to start at eight, but Gregg was receiving his guests for drinks in the Red Drawing-room an hour earlier. Not wishing to face him for the first time alone, Susan had asked Jonathan to knock at her door, and escort her—though she had not told him the real reason for it.

When she stepped in front of the gilt-framed cheval mirror for a last-minute check, she was sure she had never looked more beautiful. There was no point being falsely modest about her appearance. Tonight of all nights, she needed to boost her morale. Her hair, softly swept back from her face, but with tiny tendrils curling around her forehead and cheeks, looked more silver-gilt than gold. Nervous apprehension had darkened her eyes and made them look larger than ever, while the same apprehension had given pink to the skin that moulded her cheekbones. She wore more make-up than usual, accentuating the tilt of her eyes with mauve shadow, and outlining the soft contours of her mouth with shimmering lipstick.

Her dress was of lavender silk taffeta, a colour that gave her skin an iridescent quality. It had a low camisole bodice that outlined the full curve of her breasts, and a long, full skirt in matching layers of tulle, sashed in shocking pink. Around her throat she wore a choker, beaded in the same dazzling colour, which drew attention to the lovely curve of her neck, and with little need to enhance her appearance further, her only jewellery was a slender silver bracelet, and small silver earrings in the shape of a rose.

When she opened the door to Jonathan, he stared at her for a moment without speaking, his eyes saying all she needed to know.

'You look stunning,' he commented finally. 'Every woman will envy you, and every man will envy me.'

Every man but one, Susan thought silently, as she walked down the Long Gallery, wishing she were anywhere but here. What on earth had possessed her to come? A sudden feeling of panic as they neared the reception area almost made her turn tail and run, and it was only Gerry Rosen, calling to attract her attention at the top of the staircase, who saved her from making a complete fool of herself.

'Lovelier than ever,' he greeted her, before introducing the slim, attractive brunette at his side as his wife.

While he and Jonathan became acquainted, as they queued behind other guests waiting to be announced by the liveried footman, standing in the doorway of the drawing-room, Susan talked to Ann Rosen.

'Are you here on business or pleasure, or both?' Susan asked curiously.

'Oh, purely pleasure. Gregg wanted us all to see the house and estate, and of course, this provided a wonderful opportunity to see it at its best.'

'All?' Susan questioned.

'Gregg's family,' Ann explained. 'His mother and his three sisters and their husbands flew over with us yesterday.'

'How nice,' Susan murmured. 'How long are you staying?'

'The whole trip is rather vague. Gregg planned and paid for it all, and refuses to discuss the arrangements. But if the hints he's been dropping are anything to go by, I think we're here for something pretty special.'

'There were rumours in the papers that he's going to marry,' Susan said, and felt her heart begin to pound as she waited for Ann's confirmation.

But the footman enquiring her name prevented it, and as Jonathan lightly propelled her forward into the

Red Drawing-room, the pounding of her heart became an uneven tattoo.

So named because of the exquisite embroidered silk covering the walls and the long windows, it was more than sixty feet in length, and had a magnificent white carved and gilded ceiling. The furniture, which had been pushed back against the walls was French, the carpet Aubusson, while the paintings were Impressionist—Sisley, Manet and Renoir.

Gregg was standing just to the right of the doorway, with a woman who looked to be in her early sixties at his side—slim, with small, neat features and light brown hair, greying at the temples. Susan immediately recognised her as his mother, from the photos she had seen in the papers.

'I've heard so much about you, Susan,' she said in a soft drawl. 'But I have to say you're even more beautiful than Gregg led us to believe.'

'What more can I add to that?' Gregg said silkily, and smiled at her.

He looked incredibly handsome in his dinner jacket. It was fashionable, in the style of the twenties, and the stark black against the white winged collar of his starched shirt highlighted his smooth, tanned skin. He looked completely at ease, and somehow younger, as if a weight had been lifted from his shoulders—as no doubt it had, with his final decision to marry Davina.

Susan made a brave effort to smile back, hoping she did not look as near to tears as she felt.

'How are the bookings coming along?' she asked, for want of something to say.

'We're full for the whole of the summer season, and have a waiting list for next year too,' he replied cheerfully, before turning away with a murmured apology to greet Ann and Gerry Rosen, who had just been announced.

'Champagne, madam?' a white-coated waiter enquired at Susan's elbow.

Glass in hand, Jonathan a pace behind her, she wended her way to the centre of the room where the firm's two senior partners were standing with their wives. Grey-haired, plump and matronly, they could have been taken for sisters, and indeed were great friends.

'He's quite the best-looking man I've ever seen,' Hazel Forbes said, indicating Gregg with her hand. 'And charming too. Not at all how I'd imagined he would be.'

'The whole family's charming,' Eileen Maddox added. 'Have you met his sisters yet?'

'No, just his mother,' Susan replied.

'They're in the far corner, talking to the Duchess and some of her friends,' Eileen Maddox told her.

Susan turned her head, but it was not easy to see clearly in the rapidly filling room, bustling with staff dispensing drinks and hors d'œuvres.

'I hear there's going to be a fireworks display,' Stanley Maddox spoke. 'It's fortunate we're spending the night here, as it's taking place after midnight—way past our normal bedtime, isn't it, Eileen dear?'

This remark started a discourse on husbands falling asleep in front of the television, and after politely listening for a few minutes, Susan decided she would not be missed, and moved away to join Gerry and Ann Rosen.

'I'll see you later,' she said to Jonathan. He had declined to join her, having spotted one of the firm's client's—a leading industrialist—on the other side of the room.

'I must introduce you to Gregg's sisters,' said Gerry, almost immediately 'They're longing to meet you.'

Not giving her time to wonder why, he propelled

her across the room to where they and their husbands were standing.

It was embarrassing to be the focus of so much attention, as they fussed over her, and showered her with compliments. Only Davina stood silent, though she did manage to force a smile to blood-red lips, that not only matched the rubies at her throat and wrists, but her figure-hugging strapless dress.

The three girls and their husbands were typically American—friendly and gregarious—and after half an hour Susan felt as if she'd known them for years.

'What will you be doing now that Gregg's sold the magazine?' Susan asked Chuck Walters, Gregg's eldest sister's husband, who had handled all *Playmate*'s advertising.

'I have a service contract for the next five years with the new owners,' he smiled, 'with an option for the following five, so I guess I don't have to worry for a while yet.'

'Does that apply to Bob too?' she asked, referring to the middle sister's husband, who had also worked for Gregg.

'Yes. Emco,' he named the publishing company— one of America's largest—who had bought the magazine, 'wanted *Playmate* so badly they would have agreed to almost any conditions Gregg wanted to impose. We even have stock options as a bonus. He's quite a guy, my brother-in-law.' He smiled affectionately. 'One hell of a businessman, and a heart as big as his bank balance!'

'Which after paying for this holiday will be considerably depleted!' Gregg, who had come up behind them, had obviously overheard Chuck.

'Is everyone here, darling?' Davina addressed Gregg.

'According to the security guy at the door, we're about a dozen short.'

'Then why don't we move into the ballroom, and

open the dancing?' Davina asked, linking her arm possessively in his.

'Because I've promised the first dance to my mother,' he answered silkily, and gently extricated himself from her grip. 'But looking as lovely as you do tonight, I'm sure you'll have no difficulty finding another partner.'

A smile touched the rosebud lips, but did not reach her eyes. 'I should have guessed, darling. You're always so thoughtful towards her.'

As if on cue, the sound of the orchestra could be heard playing 'Let's Face the Music and Dance,' and moving to his mother's side, Gregg led the way into the ballroom.

It was probably the most famous room in the house, though famous not for its size, but for its beauty— octagonal in shape, bevelled mirrors inset into intricately carved panels of silver and blue, depicting cherubs intertwined with musical instruments and flowers lined the walls, reflecting many times over the crystal chandeliers and wall-brackets, which though now lit by electricity, still had candles resting in their original holders. Stools and chairs covered in silver and blue brocade were banked against the walls, and instead of curtains at the long, arched windows, there were shutters in the same two colours, drawn back to reveal the intricate delicacy of their mouldings.

'Breathtaking, isn't it?' Susan said to Jonathan, as he took her into his arms, and she would have added romantic too, but she did not wish to put any ideas into his head.

As they moved around the floor, she was able to admire the glittering, jewelled assembly, the women bright as peacocks in coloured silks and chiffons— several like her own she recognised as Bellville Sassoon—their scents rivalling those of the flowers. The men were almost as colourfully dressed, though not quite so elegant, in a variety of dinner jackets from wine velvet to green and blue brocade, that did not always flatter the more portly among them.

There were several other unattached men besides Jonathan, and during the first part of the evening Susan found herself whirled around the floor ceaselessly. In spite of herself, she could not help keeping a watchful eye on Gregg. He danced with Davina, but only for a very short time, and she assumed that the partners he chose were the wives of his friends. Certainly he tried to spread himself around, giving one duty dance after another, so that he was never with the same woman for long.

Supper was served in the State Dining-room, which was also the larger of the two in the house, and noted mainly for the tapestries at either end of the room, Beauvais and Gobelin respectively.

Long tables had been set against the walls, and the buffet was sumptuous enough to set before a king— smoked salmon, caviar, oysters, lobsters, huge Dublin Bay prawns, asparagus, turkey, duck, fillet of beef— roasted to a delicate pink perfection—and every kind of salad imaginable. There was also a hot table, with both fish and meat dishes. Desserts were equally numerous and mouth watering, and of course, champagne flowed throughout, as it had since the beginning of the evening.

Momentarily Susan was struck by pangs of conscience as she thought of the poverty of the Third World, many of whose families would be happy to subsist for a week on the food she and the other guests were consuming for dinner. She looked at Gregg, moving from group to group, playing host to perfection, looking completely at ease in his sur- roundings. Certainly he appeared to have adapted himself to Brocklehurst as to the ducal manor born. Yet he would not surprised to hear how she felt, for he too had a conscience about having so much. That was the reason he had behaved with such generosity towards the tenants. He was an excellent employer too, for she had heard he had given all the staff a large rise since taking over.

'What dark thoughts are you having to make you look so serious?' her companion, the son of a neighbouring landowner, asked.

'The only serious thought in my head is whether to have another piece of mille-feuille, or try the chocolate baskets filled with strawberries,' Susan smiled.

'Both would solve *all* your problems,' he smiled back at her, and took her plate. 'Allow me.'

She watched until he was swallowed up in the crowd, then catching Gregg's eyes upon her, and guessing his intention, helped herself to another glass of champagne from the tray of a passing waiter. She was going to need it, for he was threading his way purposefully towards her.

'Drowning your sorrows?' he asked as he drew level. He touched her arm, and his fingers on her skin sent an electric shock through her, reminding her to be on her guard.

'Hardly. I've never been happier.'

'Don't tell me you haven't missed me?' One thick blond eyebrow was raised in mock horror.

'About as much as you've missed me,' she said flippantly.

His eyes lingered on her. 'I only hope that's true, then the evening will turn out to be quite perfect.'

'Still the same faithless Gregg. You can't resist flirting, can you?'

'Faithless?' he drawled. 'Faithless to whom?'

For answer Susan let her eyes move to Davina, who was standing talking to Stanley Maddox.

'You still believe everything you read about me in the papers, then?'

Before she could reply, Chris Rawlings, her partner, returned with her dessert plate. Gregg stayed, chatting amiably for a few minutes longer, and then moved away.

'Nice chap,' Chris commented. 'We were all a bit worried when we heard he'd inherited the place, being an American and a bit of a playboy. Didn't think he'd take his responsibilities seriously. But the general consensus is that he's doing a damn fine job.'

The string quartet which had been playing in the ante-room adjoining was now replaced by the more strident beat of Latin-America from the ballroom.

'How about giving it a whirl?' Chris asked.

During the next hour or so Susan danced with Gerry Rosen, as well as Gregg's three brothers-in-law, and she could not resist the temptation of trying to pump them about his marriage plans. But they were extremely noncommittal—so much so, she suspected they had been primed by him.

When the band changed over again, there was a slight lull, and Gregg appeared at her side once more.

'Now I can concentrate on you,' he said. 'I've done all my duty dances and I won't be missed.'

'As we're not going anywhere, you certainly won't,' she said with asperity, as he put his hand around her waist and tried to propel her towards the doorway.

'Would you like me to pick you up and carry you out?' he asked. 'Because if you argue with me, that's exactly what I'm prepared to do.'

From the glint in his eye and the determined thrust of his chin, she was frightened to put him to the test by refusing.

'Your bedroom or mine?' he asked, as they walked out of the ballroom, and into the corridor. 'And don't jump to the wrong conclusion. I simply want to talk to you undisturbed, and people are wandering in and out of the other reception rooms.'

'We could go outside?' she suggested.

'Dressed like that?' he said dismissively. 'I don't want you giving me the cold shoulder, for no other reason than that you're freezing!' There was amusement in his voice, but it did not reach his eyes. They were dark blue, and she could not see the pupils.

'We'll make it your bedroom, then,' he said, taking matters into his own hands.

With a shrug, Susan acquiesced, and they walked towards it in silence. When they reached the door, Gregg waited for her to precede him, then closed it firmly behind him.

'I want to talk about the last time we saw each other,' he said immediately.

'If you want to apologise, there's really no need. I've forgotten all about it.'

'Like hell you have,' he said in a harsh voice. 'But as it happens that's only part of it.'

She placed her purse down on the bedside table and seated herself on one of the occasional chairs.

'Is this going to take long?' she asked, trying to sound indifferent.

'Only as long as it takes to convince you that I love you.'

Susan was afraid she had not heard properly, and mutely went on looking at him.

Reading her strained expression correctly, he repeated what he had said. 'I love you, Susan.' He came closer to her, but kept his hands at his side. 'I love the way you look, the way you think, everything about you.'

'I—I . . .' She moistened her lips, but before she could say anything he was speaking again.

'You're not going to deny you love me too?'

His confession that he loved her was the one thing in all the world she had wanted to hear, and she had no intention of denying her own feelings. But he had a good deal of explaining to do before she could forgive him for all the heartache of the past few months.

'No, I'm not,' she said softly. 'But why has it taken you until now to realise it?'

'I knew it months ago, but it took your accident to finally make me admit it to myself—and to your mother,' he added.

'My mother!'

'Yes.' For the first time he smiled. 'When you were so ill, I had a long talk with her.'

This explained why her mother had looked so surprised when Susan had told her Gregg intended to marry Davina. 'But why didn't she tell me?' Susan demanded. 'Why did she let me——'

'Because when you constantly refused to see me, or talk to me, I grew angry, and decided to go back to the States. I looked on it as a kind of reprieve—a chance that out of sight would be out of mind, and that I'd be able to return to my old philandering ways.' He ran his fingers through his hair. 'But I couldn't. However hard I tried, it only seemed to make me realise how much I loved and wanted *you*, to the exclusion of everyone and everything else.' His voice grew lower, and the words were fast and unmonitored, as if he wanted to get them quickly over with. 'Why do you think I sold *Playmate*? To prove, my darling, that that part of my life is over—over for ever, and a new one beginning with you.'

For an instant Susan was filled with joy. Then logic returned and she made a disclaiming gesture.

'Did you take Davina to America with you to help you forget me?'

His eyes did not flicker, but regarded her steadily. 'That was pure coincidence. She was going to Los Angeles to visit friends for Christmas, and I could hardly say no when she suggested we flew over on the same plane.' He hesistated, but only momentarily. 'I don't deny I had an affair with her. But it was brief, and I never seriously contemplated marriage to her. I only said that in the hope it would make you jealous enough to . . .' He closed his eyes, as if to blot out the memory, and even when he reopened them, they looked unseeing. 'When I could no longer make love to Davina, I had to make an excuse, but I think she guessed the real reason for it. But she went on hoping that if I could get you out of my system, I'd turn to her. That was why she told me those lies about you and Charles.'

If they were to have a future together, there had to be no secrets, no suspicions that in time to come might throw a shadow of doubt on their love.

'But you believed her?'

'What I felt for you was turning my whole world upside down, making a mockery of everything I'd always professed to be against. In my confusion and anger, I wanted to hurt you, wanted to believe you weren't perfect, that there was a flaw.'

'I'm not perfect, Gregg,' Susan protested. 'For God's sake, don't put me on a pedestal.'

He did not answer, but caught hold of her hands and pulled her out of the chair and into his arms. Never had she been more conscious of his strength, or his tenderness, as he held her close, held her as if he never wanted to let her go. 'I love you,' he groaned. 'And to me you are perfect.' His breath was warm on her cheek, his lips soft against the side of her mouth. 'I've made you suffer, but I'll do everything in my power to make it up to you.'

'Knowing you love me has done that already,' she whispered. 'Kiss me, Gregg. Show me how much you want me.'

Her arms lifted to cup his head, twining her fingers through his thick, springy hair. She pulled his face down until she could rest her lips on his, giving a soft cry of pleasure as she felt the warm pressure of his mouth.

'To do that properly would take all night,' he murmured against her lips.

'What a wonderful thought!' Susan sighed. 'And you did say no one would miss you now.'

He drew back a little and she saw the blue of his eyes had intensified and deepened, and she had the feeling that he was drawing the sight of her into the very depths of his being.

'Do you really mean that, Susan? You're willing to——'

'As I've never been willing to with any other man,' she confessed, her voice a thin thread of sound. 'You'll be the first, Gregg, and the last.'

He looked shaken. 'And to think that I . . .' He gathered her close to him again. 'No wonder you looked so scared.'

'I'm not scared any more,' she said softly. 'Make love to me, Gregg.'

A tremor ran through him, and she knew a sense of power that she was capable of doing this to him in spite of all his previous experience. His hand moved to the zip of her dress, and she closed her eyes. But suddenly he pulled away and glanced down at his watch.

'The fireworks,' he said surprisingly. 'Come to the window.'

'Darling, I——'

'Don't argue!' Catching hold of her hand, he ignored her attempted protest, and drew her towards the window.

Although puzzled at his insistence, Susan did not question it. She was too happy to think of anything but the fact that Gregg loved her.

Arms around each other, heads touching, they watched the colourful and dazzling display. But even when it had finished, he still did not move away. Instead he turned to look at her, and his expression, which though tender, was unexpectedly serious.

'I've answered all *your* questions, Susan, and now I have one of my own. I want you to promise to give me a *straight* answer for once, because it means everything to me.'

Before he could tell her what the question was, her attention was attracted by a burst of Roman candles, and etched against the midnight blue of the sky, she saw letters slowly begin to form.

I-L-O-V-E-Y-O-U-S-U-S-A-N-W-I-L-L-Y-O-U-M-A-R-R-Y-M-E?

Once again Gregg turned to face her, and though the happiness and love in her eyes spelled out her answer as clearly as the question, she did not hesitate to express it verbally.

'Oh yes, Gregg. When?'